Adelaide Florence Samuels

Daisy Travers, or, the Girls of Hive Hall

Adelaide Florence Samuels

Daisy Travers, or, the Girls of Hive Hall

ISBN/EAN: 9783337204822

Printed in Europe, USA, Canada, Australia, Japan

Cover: Foto ©Andreas Hilbeck / pixelio.de

More available books at **www.hansebooks.com**

THE *MAIDENHOOD SERIES.*

DAISY TRAVERS;

OR,

THE GIRLS OF HIVE HALL.

BY

ADELAIDE F. SAMUELS,

AUTHOR OF "DICK AND DAISY STORIES," "DICK TRAVERS ABROAD," ETC.

BOSTON:
LEE & SHEPARD, PUBLISHERS.

NEW YORK:
CHARLES T. DILLINGHAM,
1876.

Electrotyped by C. C. Morse & Son, Haverhill, Mass.

CONTENTS.

7

CHAPTER XVII.

CHAPTER XVIII.

CHAPTER XIX.

DAISY TRAVERS.

CHAPTER I.

HIVE HALL, AND HOW IT CAME TO EXIST.

WHAT a bright, sunshiny morning it was! and what a curious, prying thing the sun is, anyhow! How it did try to squeeze the whole of itself into Hive Hall school-room on this particular morning. It could not, of course, but so much of it never succeeded in getting in before. It was all over the room, in squares, angles, and bars, and every shape you could think of. Doubtless it knew that this morning Daisy intended to make her first speech to the twenty-five children who were watching her so curiously, as she stood in a great patch of sunshine upon the platform. It was well for her, that the sun did shine; a cloudy morning

11

would have lowered her spirits, and perhaps, deprived her of the courage to say what she wanted to.

Daisy Travers was the adopted grand-daughter of a wealthy old man, named Milly, who looked upon her as perfection, and who would no more have thought of refusing to comply with any of her whims, than he would have forgiven any one for underrating her beauty or goodness.

She was nearly sixteen; small, but faultless in form; with a sad, sweet face, deep blue eyes and hair— well, it was light, long and naturally curly; poor words to express all its beauty.

Her short struggle with poverty had awakened in her a sympathy for the poor, that few girls of her age can understand. Her last charitable whim, the founding of Hive Hall, was one that would be likely to cause her much trouble, and anxiety, but if carried bravely through, her compensation would be evident. The twenty-five children before her had been taken from miserably-conducted country poor-houses, and bound to grandfather Milly: why they were there we will let Daisy tell.

" You are all here, at last: " said she, flashing a glance over the faces before her: " and now I am going to tell you *why* you are here; but first I will tell you a true story that you will all be able to understand. Once upon a time there was a very little girl who lived with her father, and mother, and brother, in a country town, not a great many miles from here. She was a very happy little girl. All of you, I am sure, know what it is to be happy. Just think of some time when you were very happy, indeed, then believe that this little girl was just so happy all the time, until one day her father died; very soon after that her mother died also, and she was told that her brother would have to leave her, and go out into the world to seek his fortune, while she, all alone, must go to the poor-house. Then was ever there such an unhappy little girl as she. She had heard such dreadful stories about that poor-house. She would never be able to sleep there, she knew, but would lie every night with her eyes wide open, waiting for something dreadful to happen. She was so frightened, and cried so at the thought of going there, that at last her brother resolved to take her with him, and they would seek their fortunes together. Then in her great joy, she thought of those less fortunate than she, and made a vow to herself that if it was ever in her power to make even a few of them happy, she would do it," here Daisy paused to take breath. Twenty-five pairs of eyes, were fixed earnestly upon her face, but she did not feel now as though they belonged to strangers; no, they belonged to those whom she had thought of, and planned for, in her mind for months, and years. " They were very fortunate, this brother and sister," continued Daisy. " They were soon adopted by a good man, who proved to be very rich, and became so fond of his adopted grand-children that he would deny them nothing they might ask of him. So it was now in this girl's power to perform what she had vowed to do. Her good fortune did not make her forget that vow, you will believe, when I tell you that I am that girl, and have gathered you here to befriend you. This, henceforth will be your home, and I will try to make it all that a home can be. You have all of you, I think, seen girls and boys whom you have envied; they were well clad, while you were in rags; they were well fed, while you were hungry; they were petted, and rewarded, and Santa-Claus never forgot them Christmas time. Henceforth you will be well clad, well fed, petted, and rewarded, and Santa-Claus will never forget to -visit Hive Hall." How the sun did rush into the room! One would think all the children were sun-struck, they sat so still; and how it did make their eyes shine, as they listened to Daisy.

"I will do everything that can be done for you," continued she, "and all I ask in return is, that you will love each other, and me, as I shall love you; and that you will honestly try to do the best you can, always. If you will do that, I shall have cause to be proud of this school, and I want to be proud of it. I want to see you grow up into men and women that anyone would be proud to know. I want to be able to say one of these days, when some one is telling me about a great man, and his works, — 'why, that's one of my boys!' and when I hear every one talking about some woman, who is making a glorious name, I want to be able to say, 'yes, she is one of my girls!' But more than all, I want to know that you are every one good, and true: I want to feel always that I can trust you; then I can pity the world if it should never know you. Now, boys and girls, if you feel like giving three cheers for Hive Hall, you need not be afraid of making a noise," and Daisy smilingly withdrew, just in time to escape the full sound of such a cheer! The like was never uttered by twenty-five pauper children before.

"She shall have cause to be proud of me!" exclaimed one bright boy, looking with much satisfaction upon his neat clothes.

"And me!"

"And me!"

"And me!" sounded from every side of the room.

"Don't make fools of yourselves!" petulantly exclaimed the girl who had come the very first day. "Just keep still, and see what she wants of us. I've heard fine talk before. It's my opinion she's something like crazy Bet, where I came from. 'Dora,' she'd say to me, 'Dora, your dress is 'bout gin out, that's a fac,' Dora!" Then she'd go on to tell how I'd soon have a new one, and she'd get it for me, if I'd only get the key to the store-room, and go in, an' steal her some tea an' sugar. If I stole tea an' sugar for her once, I stole it a hundred times, but all the dress I ever got was made out of a meal-bag."

"But you have one now?" said the boy who spoke first.

" Yes, an' it's such a dreadful good one I can't get it through my head what she'll expect me to do for it. Shouldn't wonder if she wanted me to steal all-out-doors, for this dress."

"I don't believe she'll want us to steal. She is good, I know, for she talks just the way my mother did, ever so long ago, before she died," spoke up a pale-faced girl, of seven years, or thereabouts.

" Besides she is rich, and what should she want us to steal for. She isn't like your crazy Bet. She can buy any thing if she wants it! " argued the first speaker.

" I've seen rich people before to-day, I guess. It was only last summer that a rich lady came to me, an' wanted me to pick her some barberries to preserve. I was two days pickin' um, an' scratched the skin all off my hands.. *She* said she'd give me a new dress for um, but she never did, an' she kept my box, too, that I picked um in. You can't tell me any thing about rich folks."

" You came here first, didn't you? Well, has she ever treated you bad, or asked you to do any thing that was mean? " questioned the first speaker, while the other children, who were

2

beginning to forget Daisy's speech, listened attentively.

"No, she never did, as yet, that's what makes me think it'll be a regular 'stonisher when it does come. I'd do a good deal to keep these fine clothes, an' live as I have for the last two weeks, but I can tell you I'd feel safer with crazy Bet, any day."

"Say, Dora, what do they want such a thick table for?" questioned an intelligent looking girl who stood near the one addressed, pointing at the piano. "It looks to me as though it was hollow. They'll lock some of us up in it, some day, I'll bet."

"That ain't a table," replied Dora, "that's a hand-organ. I saw one at that rich lady's house, I was telling about. They can make music come out of it."

One little fellow was about to inform them that it was a piano, when the door opened, and the teacher, followed by Daisy, entered the school-room. She, the teacher, was a pleasant-faced, middle-aged woman, to whom Daisy had become already very much attached.

"This is Mrs. Burns, your teacher," said Daisy, addressing the scholars. "She is going to tell you now how she intends to teach you."

" Perhaps you had better tell them ; I am sure you can make them understand better than I can," said Mrs. Burns, to Daisy.

"Very well, then ; sit down ; or first let me have a piece of chalk, if you have some handy, and I will try to illustrate my meaning on the black-board." The chalk was soon in Daisy's hand. " Now I will draw you a picture of one kind of a teacher, and the way she teaches," said she, turning to the board. " I will first draw a ladder, which we will call the ladder of learning. I will now draw a picture of a little child just ready to step upon the first round of the ladder ; and here's another child half through school, or half way up the ladder. Now I draw a picture of the teacher — not *your* teacher, remember — who comes up with spectacles on, and a stick in her hand, and falls to beating the two children as they go up the ladder. How she makes her stick fly. The children don't want to go up now, but she makes them ; she wont let them stop to take breath ; and if they manage wearily to climb a round or two faster than usual, that is an encouragement for her to

beat the harder, until they reach 'the top; and
then they are so tired, and glad to be through
with it all, that, instead of striking out to the
right, or the left, they tottle over on the other
side of the ladder, fall down, and forget nearly
all they have learned. Now I'll draw a picture
of *your* ladder, and the way you are going up
it. There it is, and you can just imagine that
you are all of you here at the foot, ready to
take your first step up. Here stands Mrs. Burns.
She hasn't any stick in her hand, but her hands
are ready to help you up; and here is something
hanging from this first round that's worth climbing for. It will take just three months to climb
the first round. At the end of that time we will
have a holiday, and the boy and girl who have
had the most perfect lessons, in those three
months, shall receive a prize; but there are some
of you who will deserve a prize, because you
will work for it as hard as the one who will
get it, and will lose it only because you have
not the power to remember your lessons as well
as the lucky one; and so, that you may all
stand on equal ground, I have decided to give
out two prizes, just alike, to the girls, and two
to the boys: one for perfect lessons, and the

other for good conduct. Now, I will show you
what the prizes will be, and you can decide for
yourselves if they are worth striving for." So
saying, Daisy left the school-room, but soon
returned, holding in her hands a perfect little
ship, two feet in length; and, to judge from the·
exclamations of the boys, as she carried it among
them, for their inspection, they thought it would
be worth striving for.

"These sails can be furled, and here is an
anchor that will be strong enough to hold it in
a gale. I have another ship, just like this one,
for the other prize, and there is a beautiful pond,
not far from here, where the two boys who get
them, may sail them, without danger to themselves. I am very curious to know which two of
all these boys, will get them. Mrs. Burns, will
you show the girls what their prize will be?"
continued Daisy, addressing the teacher.

"Certainly," was the reply, and Mrs. Burns
left the room. Returning in a few minutes, she
caused a great excitement among the girls, for
in her arms was the most wonderful doll they
had ever seen. It had real hair, and eyes that
would open and shut; and was dressed so handsomely. But that was not all. The cunningest

little trunk, with a lock and key, and full of more clothes for dollie, made the prize complete. Mrs. Burns took out all the dresses, and exhibited them, then folded them away again in the trunk, and turned the key in the lock; not omitting to say that there was another doll and trunk exactly like that she had in her hand; and at the end of three months, the girl who had learned her lessons the best would receive one, and the girl who had behaved the best would receive the other. Then Daisy and the teacher went out with the prizes, and left the scholars for a while, that they might have a talk about them.

"Now, what do you think about it, Dora?" questioned three or four girls, as soon as they had gone.

"It's dreadful queer, any way."

"Perhaps you think she'll want you to steal 'all-out-doors,' now?" questioned the boy who had been the first to speak before, and whose name was Edgar Ford.

"I will tell you what crazy Bet would say she will want me to do, if she was here."

"What would she?"

"Why, she'd pull her white hair all down

over her face, then she'd say, 'I tell you what, Dora, she'll want you to go up and bring down the moon, then she'll want you to drive the man out of it with a broom-stick. Then she'd, crazy Bet would, tell me not to do it, because she tried to do it once, herself, an' the moon rocked over on her. That's how she came to be moon-struck."

"Are you going to try to get one of the dolls?" interrogated a small girl who stood near her.

"Land, no! I couldn't get a lesson an' I couldn't behave. But I should like to get it, just to break its head open, to see what makes its eyes open an' shut. It's dreadful queer how it does that."

"Oh-o-o!" groaned all the girls. "Break that beautiful doll!"

"What's it good for, anyhow!"

"Don't tell her! Don't have any thing to say to her!" exclaimed a quiet-appearing girl, named Anne Porter, indignantly.

CHAPTER II.

DORA'S CURIOSITY.

RESENTLY the dinner bell sounded, and the children were not slow to accept the invitation to that meal. In a wonderfully short space of time, they were all in the dining-room, enjoying themselves as only those who know what it is to be hungry, can enjoy themselves when a good meal is put before them.

Grandfather Milly was there, trotting up and down between the long tables, "seeing," as he said, "if the children knew how to eat." He decided they did, and that was the only thing they did know.

After dinner the children had permission to go out of doors, or amuse themselves in their own rooms or in the school-room, as it was Saturday, and work would not really begin till the next Monday morning.

24

It was such a pleasant day, nearly all preferred to go out of doors. Dora was the only one who returned to the school-room.

The sun had nearly gone. Two or three rays remained upon the front desks, as though to watch Dora. On entering, she closed the door after her, then seated herself on the step of the platform, and placing her chin in her hands, rested her elbows upon her knees. For a long time she sat perfectly still, looking straight before her. Then she turned her head, and her gaze rested upon the piano. After looking at it for a few minutes, she arose and approached it. Then a careful survey of all its parts followed. Doubtless she was looking for the *handle*, to turn it, as she had seen organ-grinders turn the handle of an organ; but of course her search was fruitless, and she soon turned from it in disgust, and approached the teacher's desk; this she tried to open, but it proved to be locked. Stepping down from the platform she walked to a window, and looked down upon the children who appeared to be enjoying themselves in the yard below. For a while they claimed her attention, then she discovered that she was very near the door through which Daisy and the teacher had carried the prizes. Opening the door softly, she looked into the next room; no one was there. Entering, the first thing that caught her eye was a long, green pasteboard box, on a chair; this she opened immediately, and, behold! there lay the beautiful wax doll!

"Crazy Bet always said I'd be lucky some day, an' now what am I, I'd like to know?" said she aloud, taking out the doll by its pink silk sash. "Now we'll see what makes it wink. I wonder how she made it go? Oh, I see! Yes, I can do it. That's the queerest! It must look funny inside, and I'd like to see it. Perhaps I can take the head off, an' stick it on again, some way. It would be fun to fix it so only one eye'll open. Can't get the head off without breaking it all to smash, that's a sure thing; but if I had a knife or somethin', I could dig a piece out of the back, under the hair, an' it would never be noticed." With that Dora cast her eyes around the room, in search of a "knife or something," and, unfortunately, a pair of scissors were in plain sight upon the table. "Just the thing," continued she, as she took them up, and looked at them; then, seating herself in the chair, she placed the doll across her lap, face downwards, and began her operations. But she had not imagined it would be so tender, and the beautiful prize, in less than a minute, was without a head; all that remained whole of the handsome face was two glass eyes.

" January, February, March ! Won't the girls groan when they know it ? If I had a tater, or turnip, or somethin', I'd make a head an' put these eyes in." And there was something like consternation in Dora's face, as she looked at the little pile of rubbish in her lap, then held up the gaily dressed doll, which was all perfect but the head, making a happy caricature of some of our fashionable belles.

A step sounded in the school-room. Some one was there, and would discover her, with the broken doll. Quickly and noiselessly she returned it to the box, and covered it up, then she glided into a closet, and closed the door after her, just as Daisy entered the room.

" Guess they won't find out who did it just yet," said she to herself, nestling down in a dark corner. An' they can't say I did it, when they didn't see me. If they say I did, I'll say I didn't ; then they'll have to lay it to the worms. Stands to reason, worms will eat a doll's head off if it's kep' in a box for three months; they'd eat mine off in half that time."

"Why," exclaimed Daisy, aloud, for it was she who entered the room, "I thought that doll had been put away. I'm glad the girls didn't come in here, for I don't want them to see it again till it's given as a prize. There's the key left in the closet door, too! How careless!

"Oh, she's goin' to lock me in, is she? Not if I know it," thought Dora, and stepping out of the closet, she astonished Daisy, by suddenly appearing at her side.

"Why, how you startled me! I did not hear you come in."

"Can I do any thing for you?" questioned Dora, looking at the box.

"Yes, if you want to," replied Daisy, surprised at the question, coming from one of her most doubtful pupils, and very glad to encourage the feeling that she thought had prompted it. "You can take that box and put it on a shelf in this closet. I'll open the door for you. Be very careful, because there is something in it that will break, if you let it fall."

"Oh, I shan't let it fall," replied Dora, ready to laugh aloud at her own smartness, as she took up the box and carried it to the closet. But fortune was against her, that day. On lifting up the box, one end of it hit the shelf, and down it fell, but she managed to catch it before it touched the floor.

" There !" exclaimed Daisy, in dismay, as she saw it falling.

" It didn't hurt it any, I caught it," said Dora, hastily placing it upon the shelf.

"No, it could not have got broken. The prize doll is in it. Perhaps I should have told you before, and you would have been more careful. I think I'll see if the dress got disarranged, because it will never do to give it all rumpled up to the little girl who will work hard to get it."

"It didn't get rumpled, I know. It went straight down, an' didn't tip up a bit," said Dora, making an attempt to shut the door.

"It's always best to be sure," replied Daisy, taking down the box, and opening it.

" Why, it is broken !" she exclaimed in aston-ishment, as her eyes fell upon the headless doll.

" It did break after all; didn't it ? " said Dora, with a very emotionless face.

" Yes, but that fall never broke it, and scat-

tered the pieces about, as they are scattered
here, besides putting a pair of scissors on top.
I want you to tell me the truth, now, Dora,
without fear; have you had this doll before,
to-day ? "

" No mum," was the dogged reply.

" You are quite sure? Look me in the face
now. What? You will not? that looks bad.
Where were you when I came into the room ? "

" Down stairs."

· " With the other children ? "

" Yes mum."

" Halloo! what's all this about ? " interrogated
grandfather Milly, putting his head in at the
door. " What's the trouble ? "

" Come in, grandpa. Dora, you can go up to
your room, now, and I want you to think of
what you have been telling me. If you decide
you haven't told me everything just as you
should have done, and want to tell me, you'll
find me here till supper time."

" I didn't know but the worms might a' done
it," said Dora, looking straight into Daisy's eyes.

" What worms ? "

" The worms as eats folks after they're dead.
You see it was kinder as though it was dead
an' buried, shut up in that box."

" You can go!" said Daisy, very decidedly, holding the door open for her to pass out.

"Now what's it all about?" questioned the old man, who knew by the expression on Daisy's face that something had gone wrong.

For an answer Daisy showed him the headless doll, then repeated the conversation that had passed between herself and Dora, and told him her suspicions. Poor Daisy! she had expected sympathy, and was not at all prepared for the burst of laughter that followed.

" I did not think you could be so unkind as to laugh about any thing so serious," said she, reproachfully, and nearly ready to cry.

" Can't help it, Daisy. It's laughable to see you ready to cry over the first fib, and you are not sure yet that it is a fib, either ; it might have been the worms: ha! ha! ha! "

To this Daisy made no reply, but walked to the window, and looked out.

" Come, Daisy, I'll promise not to laugh any more. You haven't told me half yet. Are you quite sure she did it ? " said the old man, ready enough to stop, on seeing that Daisy was really very much distressed.

" I am very sure she did. I think she must

have been here before I came in. I don't see how she could have come in at the door without my seeing her; and she seemed so anxious, too, to put the box away, without having it opened."

" Why not ask some of the children if she has been with them since dinner."

"I will go and question some of them. Wait here till I come back," said Daisy, as she left the room ; returning again in less than ten minutes.

" It's just as I supposed," said she, walking to the table, and looking seriously at the broken doll. She has not been down stairs since dinner, and I know she was not in her room, because I went through all the rooms just before I came in here, to see if they were in order, and she was not there, then."

" Well, then, of course she did it, and was afraid to own to it, which is not at all surprising, considering the way she has been brought up. I should have been very much surprised if she had told the truth about it. I hope you did not expect they would all prove to be ready-made angels."

" Of course not, grandpa. I don't suppose I should have minded it so much, if it had not followed so soon after my speech. I thought that would prove forcible enough to keep them steady for the rest of the day, at least," replied Daisy, with an attempt to smile.

"I don't believe the speech was ever yet made that influenced all its hearers for a day; so don't get discouraged, so quick."

"Discouraged! Of course I am not that, only there is something about that girl that I cannot understand, and I want to understand her. I want to understand every one of them, so I shall know just how to manage them."

"You can't expect to understand them all in a day."

"I know it; but if I understand her as well as I do some of them, I should know what to do with her now, which I don't; and it will not do to let this affair rest, will it?"

"To tell the truth, Daisy, I don't know what will be the best thing to do," replied Mr. Milly, after a pause, in which, in his perplexity, he first wiped his face with his handkerchief, then rubbed it all over his head, as though his head was bald, which it was not, thereby causing it to appear as though a skein of white silk was tangled up all over it.

"Grandpa, come here!" suddenly exclaimed

Daisy, who had gone to the window, and was looking out.

"What is it?" interrogated the old man, trotting up, and looking out over her shoulder.

"Don't you see? There she is, now, racing across the yard, and screaming louder than any of them."

"Sure enough! I thought I heard you telling her to go up to her room?" Grandpa looked at Daisy, and Daisy looked at grandpa. The old man tried hard not to laugh, but he did not succeed. Indeed he looked so very comical trying not to look merry, that Daisy could not but laugh herself.

"Doesn't that prove, now, just how much that girl cares for what I say," said she, at last, turning again to the window, and watching Dora, who was now running towards a small girl, who was seated upon the grass, watching a group of children, who were playing nearer the school-house. As Dora drew near the small girl, she Dora, suddenly sprang into the air, passed over her head without touching her, and came down before her, much to the small girl's astonishment, and her own evident amusement.

"What shall I do with her, grandpa?" interrogated Daisy, after she had breathlessly watched that performance.

"I should say a little oil of birch wouldn't hurt her much, but I believe you are resolved not to use that kind of medicine. So suppose you pretend not to see her, and to-night we'll talk it over."

Daisy was in the dining-room at Hive Hall, the next Monday morning, arranging some plants in the bay-window. She had brought several pots of fuchias and geraniums, from her collection at home, for the window, and she was planting some seeds in a green box, when Dora opened the door, and Daisy called her to her.

"Now it's coming!" thought Dora to herself. "I don't care what it is, I'll steal it if I can, but I rather 'spect it'll be too much for me."

"How do the flowers look?" said Daisy, noticing her eyes rested upon them with evident curiosity.

"Han'some. I never saw any like um before."

"Do you like flowers?"

"Yes. There used to be lots in the woods back of the poor-house."

"Do you know, Dora, I have been thinking this seed is very much like you, in some respects," continued Daisy, holding up a little brown seed for Dora to see.

" Like me ? " repeated Dora, looking Daisy in the face for the first time since she entered the room.

" Yes; and I will tell you why. My brother sent me this seed from Africa, a great country, hundreds of miles from here. He wrote to me that the plant he took it from he found growing in the midst of a dense forest, where it was so crowded and overpowered by stronger, and larger plants, that it could scarcely find room enough to grow at all. It should have been a handsome bush, with many flowers all over it, whereas only two or three little branches could struggle up to the light, and on one of them was a flower, on another this little seed, which if it had been allowed to fall there, would have made even a worse bush than the other. But it was taken off and sent here, to me; and here it will have all the room it wants to grow in, all the sunshine it wants, and all the nourishment it wants. Now don't you think it will be a very queer, ungrateful seed, if it doesn't do the very best it can, to grow up into a strong, handsome bush that will bear many flowers. It would be unnatural to suppose that it won't do so well here, as it would have done there, wouldn't it?"

"Yes; but why is it like me?"

"Don't you see? Don't you think your case is very much the same? Think of that little plant, then think of yourself at the poor-house, where you were overpowered by coarse, perhaps wicked, men and women, who would have crowded you down so you would have grown up very bad indeed. But now you are here, where very much more will be done for you than will be done for that seed. Won't it be strange if you do not do as well as the seed does? Won't it be strange if you do not grow up into a good woman?"

"The seed may never come up, anyhow," said Dora, who had never heard such talk before, and did not look as if she liked it very well.

"Very true; and so may you never grow up. You may die, you know, as well as the seed; and you wouldn't want to die without ever having tried to be good, would you?"

"I'm not going to die right off."

"How do you know that? You may die within a month. You may die to-day."

"I don't want to talk any longer. I guess I'll go out."

"You may go out, but first I want to tell you one thing. If I see this seed coming up a homely, scraggy, ill-shaped plant, I shall not take much pleasure in caring for it. But if I see it come up graceful, and handsome, I shall be glad to tend it every day. So it is with you, Dora. I want to see you begin handsomely, and you can, by confessing that you broke that doll, Saturday. Don't be afraid of being punished for doing it, for you will not be. Now I will leave you; and remember, as soon as you decide that you *will* begin handsomely, come to me, and see if I am not very glad to know it," then without another word, Daisy planted the seed, and left the room.

"Gorry, how she did run on!" exclaimed Dora, drawing a long breath of relief, as soon as the door had closed after her. "She can put it stronger than crazy Bet, any day. An' she never said a word about my stealin' for her. I wonder if all she wants of me is to be good? That would be harder'n stealin'! Couldn't do it anyhow. I'm a born nuisance, everybody always said so, an' I can't help it. Crazy Bet said some folks were born poets, an' some born

painters, an' I can't think of all the ways she
said people were born, but I can remember that
I was a born nuisance, an' she said I'd ought to
be thankful for it; anyway, I can't help it. I
wonder why they don't call her Crazy Daisy
here. I'm sure she's as crazy as Bet, only I
hain't seen her tear round yet; but I guess her
turns don't come so often as Bet's did. She
looked all down to the heel, just the way crazy
Bet used to when she asked me to steal some
tea for her. I wonder, if I should tell her I
broke the doll, it would brighten her up like the
tea used to brighten up Bet. I've a good mind
to try. But I guess I'd better see how the seed
comes up first, or else she'd get mad. If the
seed comes up han'some, then I must come up
han'some; that means I must tell her I broke
the doll. Dear! dear! it's dreadful hard work
getting along with crazy folks, anyhow. But it
is ever so much better here, than it was there,
because, in the first place, if she gets tearing, I
shan't be afraid of her, 'cause she ain't big
enough to hurt anybody; then there's such a lot
to eat, an' such spankin' clothes! The only way
I could get along with crazy Bet was to agree
to everything she said. That's the way I'll have

to do with crazy Daisy, or whatever her name is. If she's very crazy, an' I think she is, now, she'll watch that seed like a cat watching a mouse, an' I'll have to watch it, too, so if it comes up han'som, I can get on her good side, by sayin' I broke the doll. But s'pose it don't come up? Then she'll say it died, an' she might try to kill me, too, 'cause she thinks I'm just like it; crazy Bet would. Guess I'll go out an' see 'f I can't hunt up some kind of seeds to stick in with that one, so something 'll come up, she'll never know the difference."

But Dora did not find any. As the days past by, she began to show considerable anxiety in regard to the seed Daisy had planted. Instead of leaving the dining-room immediately after every meal, as the other children did, she would walk up to the bay-window, to see if it had yet started from the ground. Her evident anxiety did not pass unnoticed by Daisy, who began to think her "lecture" might have done some good after all; and she was quite sure of it, when two little green leaves made their appearance in the box in the bay window, Dora came to her and said, without any prevarication, and suddenly enough to astonish Daisy:

" I did break that doll."

"I knew you did, at first, Dora, but I am very glad you have at last found courage enough to tell me so," replied Daisy; and Dora, watching her face, thought it did light up even more than crazy Bet's used to when she received the much-prized tea.

For some time Daisy talked to her very earnestly and kindly, to encourage her in well-doing, then hurried home to tell Grandfather Milly, of her "great success." If she could have known what Dora's thoughts were after she had left her.

"I knew it!" said that individual to herself, as soon as she was alone. "She's worse'n crazy Bet; but land! I know how to manage her!"

"DORA?"

"Yes, mum."

"Mrs. Burns has given me a very bad report of you."

"That's good of her. I thought she was too stingy to give anybody any thing."

"Mrs. Burns is an excellent woman, and does her duty wonderfully well. I expected better of you, after what you told me in the dining-room. It seems the seed has the most gratitude, after all. It has come up, and is growing nicely, to pay me for all the care I've taken of it; but everything I do for you seems to make you worse. Why did you pound poor Kate Wrenton, who is so much smaller than you are, so unmercifully?"

"I pounded her 'cause I couldn't help it, any more'n the seed could help coming up; but I'd

just as live ask her pardon as not, now ; bring
her here an' see if I wouldn't."

" What good would that do, now ? She will
be sore and lame for a week at least."

" It's her own fault, anyway ; she wouldn't
stop foolin' when I told her to, an' she got me
mad."

" I'm afraid you have a very bad temper
Dora."

" 'Spect I've got a pretty bad one ; but then
crazy Bet used to say that a knife or any thing
else wasn't any good 'less it had a temper."

" I don't want you to mention crazy Bet's
name again while you are at Hive Hall ! Do
you understand that ? "

" Come, now, you needn't be so hard on
crazy Bet, 'cause you're crazy yourself, you
know."

" I think I must have been very crazy,
indeed, when I took such an ungrateful girl as
you are to bring up, hoping to make a good
woman out of her," and Daisy, who could hold
back her tears no longer, sat down and began
to cry.

" Oh, come, I wouldn't do that," said Dora
Wentworth, in dismay, going up to her. " I'll

call you Aunt Daisy, if you want me to, an'
not the other name; an' I won't tell anybody I
found it out. Nobody knows it here but me,
I'm sure."

" Found what out? Knows what?" questioned
Daisy, looking at the girl before her in bewilderment.

" Oh, never mind, if you don't remember.
Isn't there something you want me to do,
now ? "

" You know very well," replied Daisy, " that
all I want you to do, is to try to be a good
girl; and you will not do that. For a punish-
ment you must remain here in my study till
bed-time. You cannot go down to supper with
the other children, but will have bread and
water here," and Daisy arose to leave the room,
thoroughly out of patience with this girl who
was sure to disturb the whole school, some way,
every day. After Daisy left the study, Dora
stood listening, till she could no longer hear her
receding footsteps, then she approached the door
with the intention of going out, also; but she
very soon discovered that she was securely
locked in.

" She did that well! " said she, at last, after

satisfying herself that the door could not be opened. " Crazy Bet would have left the door open, after that speech. She looked almost, when she went out, as if she 'wasn't crazy after all ; but then Bet used to look so, too, at times. Any way, she won't catch me again, in a hurry, as slick as she did this time. Wonder if I couldn't get out the window. Guess not — it's a leetle too high. Never mind, I haven't seen all there is to be seen here yet," so saying, Dora walked up to Daisy's writing desk, opened it, and became very much interested in its contents. After satisfying her curiosity there, she curled herself up in the easy chair for a nap, where we will leave her for a while, and follow Daisy, who, as soon as she reached home, sought her grandfather, to inform him of what had happened at the school, and ask his advice.

" What ? Dora gave a little girl a dreadful pounding ? Why, I thought you said only the other day that you had talked her into trying to be good ? "

" It was only so many words wasted. I wish you would come up to the Hall and talk to her. Perhaps she would pay more attention to you than she does to me."

" Not likely."

" But you will try, won't you? She's the strangest girl I ever saw. She seems to want to do all she can to please me while I am with her, but just as soon as she's out of my sight she forgets all her promises, and it seems as though she couldn't act bad enough."

" She isn't trying for one of the prizes, then ? "

" No, indeed. I don't believe a doll could be bought that would be handsome enough to induce her to try to win it."

" If she doesn't like dolls, why not ask her what she would like, then tell her she can have whatever she wants if she'll work for it."

" I might try that, and if it doesn't succeed in making a change in her, I'm sure I don't know what I shall do with her."

" Then keep her a close prisoner."

" I thought of that. She is locked up now, in my study."

" I'd keep her there, till she promises to do better. She mustn't be allowed to influence the other children."

" Until she promises to do better ! Oh, grandpa, you do not know her yet. If I should ask her to promise to do better, she would, without any hesitation, whatever; and in less than half an hour I would hear that she had done something dreadful, again. She is a thoroughly bad girl. Lying seems to come natural to her, and I'm sure if she liked the looks of any thing, she would not hesitate to steal it. Making allowance for the way she was brought up, it seems as though she might show a little gratitude, when she is treated well."

" Well, well, Daisy, don't get discouraged because you've got one exceedingly black sheep in your flock. She may come out all right in the end, if we can find out how to manage her."

" Are you coming up to the Hall this afternoon, grandpa?"

" Yes, I think I'll step in and take a look at your prisoner."

" I wish you would, and talk to her, too. I've used all my eloquence on her to no purpose."

" I'll go up with you, and hear what she says about something else for a prize."

" Why not come now, and stop in the schoolroom a while to see how the other scholars prosper?"

This Mr. Milly agreed to do, and they were

soon in the school-room at Hive Hall, where Daisy's charity scholars were all assembled but one.

Daisy could not help thinking that her school, so far, was a success, notwithstanding Dora, as she looked upon the children who had improved wonderfully in one short month. Grandfather Milly thought so, too, and had a smile for every child that looked up at him, as he sat in the chair on the platform, listening to a class of small scholars, who were making a dreadful piece of work of their spelling lesson.

" I will take the boy and girl, who have had the best lessons to-day, to ride in the pony-phæton, and the boy shall drive the ponies," said Daisy, just before leaving the school-room. This she always tried to do pleasant days, and found it worked wonderfully well; for very proud, indeed, · were the boy and girl who had earned the right to step into the stylish little phæton, when it stopped at Hive Hall purposely for them; and didn't they know just how the other children envied them, as they watched them ride away.

Grandpa Milly, and Daisy, after leaving the school-room, entered the study, and saw Dora, curled up in an easy chair, apparently sound asleep.

"She is asleep," said Daisy, bending over her. "She isn't a bad-looking girl, is she; what a pity she will not behave as well as she looks. Would you wake her up?" But Mr. Milly's opinion about it was not necessary, for, at that moment Dora became wide awake so suddenly, that Daisy could not help wondering if she had been asleep, or had only been feigning sleep. There was something in her eyes, as they searched Daisy's that the latter could not understand; a puzzled, questioning look, that must have been returned by one equally puzzled and questioning, but no chance for an explanation followed, as at that moment a knock was heard at the door, and opening it a very small boy wanted to know if Daisy would return to the school-room, as Mrs. Burns wanted to ask her advice about something she had forgotten to mention when she was there.

"I'll be back in a minute," said she to grandfather Milly, as she turned to go, leaving the old man alone with Dora. For some minutes they sat looking into each other's faces, without speaking a word. Grandfather Milly was the first to break the silence, by saying, sarcastically:

"You're a pretty girl, now don't you think you are?" 4

" She just said so, didn't she? an' I guess she'd ought to know. Who are you, any way? One of the overseers of the poor, I reckon."

" I don't know but I might call myself that," replied Mr. Milly, with a laugh.

" Thought so. She calls you gran'father; you are not her gran'father, are you? "

"Not her own grandfather, but—"

" She thinks you are, eh? "

" She thinks I make her a very good one."

" Does she ever git into a tantrum? "

"A what? "

" Does she ever have a turn, or tantrum, or whatever you call it."

" Never, if by that you mean to ask if she has a temper. She is always just as good and amiable as you have always seen her. Is it possible you do not understand her? "

" I guess, Mr. Overseer, I understand her just a *leetle bit* better'n you do, if it comes to that," replied Dora, sitting back in her chair, with a satisfied air, as though she had at last settled some question to her satisfaction.

" Come now, tell me what you think of her? " questioned the old man, both amused and curious.

" Wouldn't you like to have me, now? "

" Yes, very much."

" Well, I won't, then. I've seen overseers before. If she never has tantrums, it's 'cause you don't know what I do. Soon's you find that out, she'll have um fast enough, I bet. Guess I won't give you a chance to spit your spite on her, every time you get mad. While Dora was delivering this speech, grandfather Milly sat looking at her in open-mouthed astonishment ; then, with an exclamation he could not suppress, he arose to his feet, just as Daisy entered the room.

" What's the matter, grandfather ? " said she.

" I want to speak to you a minute," he replied, as he led her across the room, so that Dora might not hear what he had to say.

" What is it ? " said Daisy, looking questioningly into his face.

" I've found out what's the trouble with that girl."

" What is ? "

" She's crazy ! Mad as a March hare ! "

" Nonsense ! "

" I believe it. If you could have heard her talk just now, you'd have said so yourself."

" As though I haven't talked to her every day, since she's been here, and I never saw any signs of craziness, unless a disposition to be bad may be called that. I'm going to ask her, now, if she wouldn't rather have something else for a prize."

" Let me ask her."

" Very well, you can if you want to."

" I've been thinking," continued Mr. Milly, turning to Dora, " that perhaps the reason why you are not trying for a prize, with the other children, may be because you don't care for dolls, even if they are handsome. What would you like better ! "

" Why, I should rather have a hand-organ, if I was to have any thing."

" A what ? "

" A hand-organ. A real one, with a handle, such as I seen a man turning once."

Grandfather Milly looked at Daisy, whose eyes told him to say she might have one, if she could earn it.

" Very well, then, you shall have one if you will be a reasonably good girl for two months. On the very day the other girls receive their dolls, you shall have a hand-organ if you deserve it."

" Could I get one as easy as that ? "

" Yes."

" Land! Then I don't want one. Like as not I'd get tired of turning the old thing the first day."

" Then you won't try for any prize? "

" What do I want to try for any prize for? I'm all right. Never was so comf'table in my life," and Dora, unconscious of grandfather's suspicions, looked first at her clean hands, then at her neat, well-fitting dress, which she smoothed out with evident satisfaction.

" No, you're not right. You are all wrong, Dora," said Daisy, speaking for the first time. "I was in hopes you would try for something. I am very sorry to see you so blind to what is for your own good."

" Did *you* want me to try for a hand-organ? "

" Of course I did."

" Then I'll try, for you, truly, 'cause I like you, better'n ever I liked Crazy Bet."

" Do you really like me? "

" Yes, I do," and there was no mistaking the truth of what she said then.

" I am very glad of that because if you do really like me you will surely try to please me, and earn a prize, won't you? "

" Jus' see 'f I don't."

"I cannot put much faith in your promises. You said you would try to be good before."

"An' I did try."

"But if you do not try harder, you cannot have the hand-organ, and will have to be a prisoner in this room every day, until you do try; how would you like that?"

"Why, that would be fun, if you'd just let me keep the key. Let's take it—won't you?"

"Certainly not. But I hope I shall not have to use it long against you."

"You might lock me in some day, an' forget all about me, 'n I'd starve to death, like 's not."

"I shall not forget you, but it will be better for you if you decide not to be locked in." At those words Dora arose and crossed the room, then beckoned to Mr. Milly to come to her.

"'Tisn't going to do," said she to him in a low tone, that Daisy might not hear. "Tisn't going to do to let her lock me up in here. I could get the key away from her, easy enough, but I might hurt her, an' I don't want to do that. Couldn't you manage to get it away from her, somehow, an' let me out?"

"I should be very glad to let you out, but it

must be as she says; when you decide to behave yourself, you are free."

" How 'm I going to try for the hand-organ, unless I'm out? "

" You can begin to try for that to-morrow, but the first time you break any of the rules, you will be locked in here again, to stay for a long time." With that Mr. Milly joined Daisy, and they left the room together, locking the door after them.

" What did she say? " questioned Daisy, while descending the stairs.

" She wanted me to get the key away from you, and let her out. She also said she could get it away from you herself, but was afraid of hurting you. She's a queer girl, any way. One minute I think she's crazy, and the next I think she's altogether too smart for us. One thing is certain, it will never do to let her be with the other children unless she improves."

CHAPTER IV.

CHERRY–STONES, AND MRS. HODGE'S METHOD.

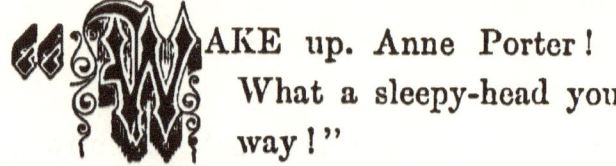 AKE up. Anne Porter! wake up! What a sleepy-head you are, any way!"

"Who is it? What's the matter?"

"Get up an' dress yourself, an' I'll tell you while you're dressing."

"Who says I'm to get up?"

"I do."

"Guess I won't get up for you, Dora Wentworth, an' I'll tell Mrs. Burns in the morning how you come into my room nights and wake me up."

"Stupid! I suppose I must tell you first, an' waste time, an' I thought you the smartest girl in the school, too, that's why I came to you. I found out something this morning that's worth knowing. In that big orchard that's next to our yard, there's the biggest cherry-tree I ever saw, an' it's just loaded down with great white-heart cherries. I couldn't get at one, 'cause there was a man watching me, as though he couldn't think what I was there for, any how. That's the beauty of being a girl! If I'd been a boy he'd have known what I was there for, fast enough, and set the dog on me. As it was, he only looked. So I thought I'd go back an' wait till night, an' get all I wanted. I'm goin' now, an' you can go with me, if you want to."

" I don't want to," was Anne's decided reply, as she nestled back under the bed-clothes.

" Why not? "

" Because, it would not be right."

" Perhaps you think if you got found out you'd lose the prize," sarcastically.

" Of course I should."

" Well, you'll lose it, any way, I can tell you that; an' you'd ought to lose it if you think an old doll is better'n one's fill of white-heart cherries. But you won't get found out. I know how to open the front door without makin' a bit of noise. Come, hurry up, an' dress, can't you? " and Dora took hold of Anne's shoulder with the intention of helping her out of bed.

" If you don't go out of my room, Dora, I'll

scream, and wake up everybody in the house; and you must promise you'll not go out to-night too, or I'll tell, as it is!"

"I always thought you was a mean old pig — now I'm sure of it. Of course I can't go unless you go, too. You see I was kinder 'fraid to go alone, on account of ghosts and goblins; but I knew if I took such a homely piece as you are, along, they'd be glad enough to keep out of our way.

"You are the very worst girl at Hive Hall! Everybody knows that."

"An' you're the worst lookin' one. I can be as good as you any day I want to; but I'd like to see you make yourself good-lookin'. You can go to sleep now, and dream of your prize; I won't trouble you again." With that Dora returned to her own room, where she seated herself at the window, and looked out into the bright moonlight, towards the orchard in which were the coveted ·cherries. Once she glanced upwards into the starry sky, and wondered if what she had heard so many times lately about God, was true. If he really did make her, and make all things, or was it all talk. Wouldn't this beautiful night be just the same without

Him? Who is He? What is she herself? were some of the questions she would have liked to have had answered to her satisfaction, just then, while looking up into the starry sky; but the next moment all such thoughts vanished as her gaze returned to the orchard.

" Just wait till she goes to sleep, an' see 'f I don't have some ! " said she to herself. "I won't be piggish, neither, see 'f I am. I'll give her a part of• all I get; yes, she shall have all the stones," and Dora could be seen smiling to herself in the moonlight. She's gone to sleep, again, by this time," continued she, after a pause. " Guess I'll try now, an' see 'f I can't get out without waking up the whole house, an' everybody in it," so saying she stole softly out into the long passage, then down the stairs, and noiselessly slid back the bolt that fastened the front door. She had no sooner closed the door softly behind her, when a white-robed figure descended the stairs, after her, and going to the door, shot the bolt in its place securely locking her out.

" There ! " said Anne to herself — for it was she — as she returned to her room. " She'll have all night to eat cherries in now, an' I hope she'll get enough of them. The hateful thing to call me homely! I wonder if she calls herself handsome, with those old goggle eyes of hers. Won't she be mad when she finds she's locked out! Now I can go to sleep with some comfort," and Anne returned to her bed in a much better frame of mind than she had been in when she left it.

In the meantime Dora had secured a seat in the cherry tree, where all the fruit she could wish for was within her reach ; and after eating all she wanted, she filled her hat full to take home to enjoy in her own room. She had been a little frightened at first, as it was the first time she had ever undertaken such an enterprise in the night ; but now, as she returned, all fear had left her, and she walked along leisurely, holding her hat full of cherries before her.

Climbing the high wall, and saving her cherries, was a difficult matter, but she accomplished the feat at last, and soon after was softly lifting the latch to the front door of Hive Hall.

" How the door sticks ! " said she to herself, after spending some strength upon it, to no purpose. " I bet it'll make a noise when I open it. Here goes, anyhow," and Dora, after placing her hat full of cherries upon the stone step, endeavored, with all her strength, to force open the door. " It's locked, as true as the world! was her next low exclamation, when her effort proved unsuccessful. " Anne Porter did that, fast enough," continued she, seating herself upon the step, and commencing to eat cherries, after a careful glance around in the moonlight. Well, she's smarter'n I thought she was, any way. I'd ought to save some cherries for her, that's a fact, to pay her for not bein' afraid to go down stairs in the dark. Wait till I get in, an' I'll reward her, see 'f I don't." With that, Dora arose to her feet, and taking up a small stone, began to knock upon the door with it.

Presently a light was visible in the house-keeper's sleeping-room, then a window was opened and " Who's there? " came down to Dora, who was concealed from view by the porch. " Who's there, I say!" was repeated in a shrill voice, but Dora remained perfectly quiet. " I think I must have been dreaming," were the next words heard, then the window was closed.

Dora remained perfectly quiet, for perhaps five minutes, then she began to tap softly upon the door again, with the stone. A few minutes

later she heard steps descending the stairs, then
she quickly picked up her hat, and crouched
close to the house, in the shadow of the porch.

Presently the door was cautiously opened. " I
don't understand it; I'm sure I heard somebody
knock," said the house-keeper, after looking out,
and perceiving no one; then she stepped softly
to the end of the house, and peered around the
corner in the direction of an old shed that looked,
in the moonlight like a lurking-place for robbers,
leaving the door open that she might retrace
her steps, at a moment's notice.

She had no sooner reached the end of the
house, than Dora darted in the door, up the
stairs, and entered her own room, where she
pushed the cherries under the bed, then jumped
into it, all dressed as she was. Fortunately for
her, her sleeping companion was a very small
girl, and a sound sleeper.

She listened and heard the house-keeper return.
A quarter of an hour passed then she arose,
and moved towards Anne's room. Anne proved
to be sound asleep.

"Land!" exclaimed Dora under her breath,
as she bent over to look at her. "She knew
I'd be back to treat her, that's why she went
to sleep with her mouth open."

" Marrow-bones, cherry-stones, bundleumjig ! "
continued she, aloud, as she dropped a handful
of cherry-stones into Anne's open mouth, then
hurried back to her own room.

Poor Anne was awake in a minute, and,
sitting up in bed, began to spit, and cough out
the stones, frantically.

" What's the matter ? " questioned her room-
mate, awaking for the first time that night, and
looking at her companion in alarm.

" I — don't know — I'm — sick. Call Mrs.
Burns — or somebody."

" What's that you're spitting out ? "

" My teeth, I guess. No, it can't be, 'cause
I can feel — them all in. It must be the croup.
People always — choke, when they have the
croup. I'm choking — to death ! *Can't* you call
somebody ! "

Lucy Stone, such was her name, rolled out of
bed. It was much easier for her to roll out
than to step out, she was so fat and round. As
she passed the window, on her way to the
teacher's room, her face could be very plainly
seen in the moonlight. She was not a homely
girl, neither was she a handsome one. Her nose
was as round as a nose could possibly be, and

her mouth was nothing but a little, round hole. Perhaps her eyes were rounder than usual, to-night, as she thought of going the whole length of the long passage in the dark, to the teacher's room frightened her a little.

Lucy was not at all smart, and would never be able to earn the prize for perfect lessons; and, though there was not a better dispositioned girl in the whole school, every one knew she would not take the prize for good behavior, as that included a neat, and orderly appearance, in regard to dress, and Lucy's toilet was always far from perfect. It was too bad it should be so, you will say, when you know that not one of the girls wanted to possess one of those beautiful dolls half so much as Lucy did.

She soon succeeded in arousing Mrs. Burns, and that motherly woman was presently bending over Anne, with a lamp in her hand.

"What's the trouble, Anne? Lucy tells me you are sick," said she.

"I think it's the croup," replied Anna in a faint voice, lying back on the pillow.

"Nonsense. I might believe that of Lucy, but you are altogether too thin, to be troubled with that disease."

" I nearly choked to death, an' lots of hard stuff come out of my mouth."

" Hard stuff ? "

" Yes."

" Where is it ? "

" It must be all over the floor."

" I don't see anything but cherry-stones." said Mrs. Burns, stooping down, and flashing the light all around.

" Cherry-stones ? " repeated Anne, sitting up quickly, and looking down at the floor.

" Where in the world did you get so many cherries ? " questioned Mrs. Burns, looking severely at her.

"I didn't get any," replied Anne, lying down again, as the truth flashed across her mind. " It's that Dora Wentworth."

" Dora Wentworth, again ? "

" Yes. She came in here a long time ago, an' wanted me to get up, an' go after cherries, in the big orchard, near here. I said I wouldn't go, an' made her promise she wouldn't, but I s'pose she did go, after all, an' when she came back, she must have come in here, an' put those stones in my mouth, when I was asleep."

Anne did not think it was necessary to say

anything about herself getting up and locking her out.

Mrs. Burns looked troubled, after hearing her explanation, and she left the room without a word.

" Did she really go after cherries, all alone in the dark? " questioned Lucy, her eyes very round, indeed, after Mrs. Burns went out.

" Dark! " repeated Anne, sarcastically. " I don't think its very dark out, do you? "

" But it's night, you know."

" What of that? "

" I don't see how she dared to do it."

" What a coward you are, anyway, Lucy," remarked Anne, all the while thinking how she felt when she went down stairs to lock the door.

" Why didn't you go with her, when she asked you, if you wasn't afraid? "

" Do you think I'd steal? "

" Oh, I forgot the cherries don't belong to us."

" You forget everything you'd ought to remember," scornfully.

" I know I do; if I didn't I'd stand a chance of getting one of those beautiful dolls. Oh, dear! I wish I could get one."

" It isn't at all likely you will; you miss, every

day, you know, and you are never half fit to be seen. I'm trying for both prizes. I don't expect to get them both, but if I should, I'd let you take one of the dolls, once in a while; an' we could play visiting with them, then."

" Oh, would you? That would be splendid. I *hope* you will get both prizes. Wouldn't it be nice to have them both here, in our room? "

" You could help me to get them, if you want to."

" How ? "

" You know it's my turn, every other day to make our bed, and sweep an' dust the room. If you'd do it every day, I'd have all that time extra to study, an' fix myself in."

" Of course I'll do it. I like to make the bed, and dust and sweep, and am always glad when my day to do it comes round. You shall have all the time to study, and fix up in, and I will help you every way I can, if you'll only tell me just what you want me to do."

" Do you know how to curl hair ? "

" Dear me ! no ; why ? "

" Because I wanted you to curl mine."

" Your hair doesn't curl, does it ? "

" No ; but I didn't know but you could make it."

"Perhaps I can; I'll try, anyway."

"If you do I'll look ever so much better and stand a better chance of getting a prize; because if I go down every morning, looking real nice, and with my hair curled, Mrs. Burns will give me a credit for it, I know." With that, Anne turned over and went to sleep, while Lucy lay awake for some time, wondering if it would be possible for her companion to take both the prizes, and hoping it would be.

The next morning Anne was awakened by feeling the fresh air from the open window blowing upon her face, and hearing a noise as if some one was sweeping the carpet, vigorously. Opening her eyes she beheld Lucy Stone, in her night-dress, and looking very warm, at that, sweeping the room.

"What in the world are you doing, so early?" said Anne, fretfully.

"It isn't very early, an' I thought if I was to try to curl your hair I'd better get this work out of the way."

"Has the first bell rung yet?"

"No, but I expect to hear it, every minute."

"I never was so sleepy in my life: but I suppose I may as well get up, now. I don't believe

we'll see Dora Wentworth in the school-room
to-day," continued Anne, looking at the cherry-
stones on the carpet, and yawning fearfully.

"I wonder what they'll do to her."

"Lock her up, very likely, as they did yesterday, an' feed her on bread an' water till she
forgets how cherries taste. It'll serve her right,
too. She's the hatefulest girl I ever set eyes
on."

"I like her. She knows a lot."

"Oh, does she! contemptuously."

"I mean compared to what I know. An'
truly, I think she might take a prize, if she
wanted to, 'cause she can remember her lessons
so easy, when she wants to. The other day
Emma Goodwin an' I were studying together,
an' she listened to us a little while. She never
looked at her own book, once, I know; an'
when she came to recite, she had her lesson
better'n either of us."

"Which isn't saying much; you two are the
worst scholars in school."

"She was always real good to me, too," continued Lucy, after a pause, in which she swept
away, aimlessly. Lots of times I don't know
that my dress isn't buttoned up straight behind,

until she comes up to me an' says, ' Rolly, you don't like black marks an' you're good for one. Stan' still while I fix you.' Then she'll button it up right for me. That's .more'n any other girl ever did for me, anyway," continued Lucy, perceiving that Anne was inclined to laugh.

" There's the first bell, now ! " exclaimed Anne, springing from bed. " Hurry up, an' finish sweepin', an' make the bed. By that time I'll be ready for you to curl my hair. It's your morning to fix the room, anyway, this morning, isn't it ? "

" Yes."

" Never mind if it isn't done very well, then, only hurry."

" I'm hurrying as fast as I can."

" That's right. I'll be ready for you, as soon as you are for me."

The first bell woke up Dora, who sprang our of bed, and began to dress, immediately. " If I thought," said she to herself, " they'd find out about the cherries I wouldn't make the bed. Oh, come to think of it, 'tisn't my morning to make it. Here, child, wake up ! " continued she, taking hold of her room-mate's shoulder, and shaking it roughly. At that moment the door opened, and Daisy Travers looked in upon her.

"Good morning," said she, turning about quickly, a little surprised at such an early visit from her. Daisy was on her way to the city, and had stopped at the Hall to give Mrs. Burns a book she had asked for the day before, and that good woman had informed her of Dora's midnight proceedings.

"I am surprised and grieved to hear another bad report of you, so soon," said Daisy, looking reproachfully at Dora, without replying to her 'good morning,' as she stepped into the room.

"What did they tell you, now? I'll bet they made it out worse than it was," replied Dora, sitting down on the edge of the bed, and casting a searching look into Daisy's eyes, which the latter could not understand. She had received that look so often of late, that it was beginning to puzzle her exceedingly, as she had noticed it was never bestowed upon anyone but herself; but she was too much offended to ask the meaning of it this morning.

"They could not have made it out much worse than it was, if it is true at all; and those cherries in your hat prove that it is."

"Have some? They're just the nicest ever

you tasted," said Dora, taking up the hat, and offering its contents to Daisy.

"I don't care for stolen fruit, and this little girl must not see them when she wakes up. Open the window and throw them out."

"Why, that would be a wilful waste, an' 'wilful waste makes woful want.' It would be woful, now, wouldn't it, to have me wanting them cherries, an' they down in the mud?"

"Let me have the hat!" and Daisy, before Dora could guess at her intention, had snatched the hat from her hand, and thrown the cherries out of the window.

"If you wasn't crazy, I'd pound you for that!" exclaimed Dora, very much excited.

"Crazy?" repeated Daisy, suddenly remembering what her grandfather had said to her the day before, then laughing at the thought, as soon as it came. "Do you think *I'm* crazy?"

"I *know* you are, an' you know it, too, if nobody else here does: an' I hope it'll make you as mad to hear me say so, as it used to crazy Bet!" and there was a half doubtful, half defiant look in Dora's eyes, as she watched the effect of her words upon Daisy.

"How long have you thought that of me?"

questioned the latter, quietly concealing her surprise.

" Ever since I've been here. S'pose I can't tell a crazy person when I've lived with one all my life ? "

" What makes you think I'm crazy? Is it because I've treated you kindly? "

" No," replied Dora, her eyes falling beneath Daisy's, " but you act an' talk at times, just as Bet used to. Perhaps you're not so far gone as she was, but you will be when you're as old."

" Did you ever know anyone that wasn't crazy ? "

" Yes."

" Name some one that you are quite sure isn't crazy."

" Mrs. Hodges, as has charge of the poor-house. No one ever said she was crazy."

" Why not? "

" Oh, because ; she was smart, she was ; she could make us all mind, even to crazy Bet herself."

" Could she make *you* mind ? "

" I used to think it would be best for me to."

" What would she do if you didn't mind."

" Make me black an' blue all over," replied

Dora, confident that Daisy wasn't large enough to prove her saneness that way, if she should try.

By this time the little girl in bed was awake, and listening to all that was said.

"Come, Maria, I want you to get up and dress yourself as quickly as you can," said Daisy to her; then taking Dora's dress, she spread it across a chair, sat down upon it, and, taking a note-book from her pocket she tore from it a leaf, and began to write something upon it with a pencil; Dora watching her curiously the while.

Presently Maria was dressed, and Daisy, giving her the paper, said:

"I want you to take that to Mrs. Shote, the house-keeper; you'll find her in the kitchen, I think. You need not come back again."

"It's my morning to make the bed, aunt Daisy," said the small girl, stopping half way to the door, on remembering that she would be likely to get a black mark, if her room wasn't in order, when the house-keeper went through the rooms, to see that everything was as it should be in them.

"Never mind. I will tell Mrs. Shote to attend to it this morning," replied Daisy, and Maria left the room, very glad to get rid of that much work, so easily.

Dora still sat upon the edge of the bed, surveying her feet, and watching Daisy, who appeared to be unconscious of her presence, as she sat drawing on her gloves.

Presently Dora stepped down upon the floor, and approached her, with:

"I'd like my dress; you're on it."

"You can't have it yet."

"I must. I want to dress myself, an' go down stairs."

"You cannot."

"Cannot? why?"

"Because, I'm going to convince you soon, by Mrs. Hodge's method, that I'm not crazy. Here is Mrs. Shote, now," continued Daisy, as the stout form of the house-keeper entered the room. "Good morning, Mrs. Shote. I see you are prompt, and understood my note," continued Daisy, as her eyes rested upon a long, thin rattan, in the house-keeper's hand. "This is the girl."

"Indeed, I m glad you've resolved to punish her, at last, Miss," said Mrs. Shote, bending the rattan between her two hands, and looking, with evident satisfaction on the consternation visible on Dora's face. " I've had four girls to bring up, an' they wouldn't have been the smart women they are now, if I hadn't used the rod on 'em pretty freely."

" How did you punish them, when they deserved it ? "

" Why, I'd just tie them to the bed-post an' belabor their shoulders well, with a stick that wasn't near so comfortable as this one."

" If Dora must be punished, and she says, herself, it's the only way to make her mind, I would rather you would punish her on her hands. If she will not submit to that, then she must be tied to the bed-post. How shall it be Dora ? " and Daisy turned, and looked into Dora's face, for the first time since the house-keeper entered the room.

Dora returned the look, with such an expression of bitter disappointment. She was convinced at last — and the knowledge was anything but pleasant to her — that Daisy was sane. As sane, even, as Mrs. Hodges; there could no longer be any doubts about it; for Bet, good old, crazy Bet, would never talk like that about having her punished; but would save her from being punished, instead, as she had often done, taking all the blame upon herself.

" What are you going to whip me for, any-how ? I don't see as I did anything very dread-ful," said she, at last, looking at the formi-dable form of Mrs. Shote, then again at the rattan in her hand.

" Hear that, now ! " said that woman, addressing Daisy, with an incredulous smile. " A girl that would get up in the dead of the night, an' walk near a quarter of a mile, to steal cherries, not to say anything of disturbing peaceable people, an' making them get up, doesn't know what she's to be whipped for ! "

" If there was any other way of convincing you that you must do better, you should not be punished that way," said Daisy, seriously. You will not listen to reason, and cannot appreciate kind treatment, and your promises to do better are worse than none. Do not wait any longer, Mrs. Shote," and Daisy, very much excited inwardly, but outwardly very calm, motioned for Mrs. Shote to begin, then walked to the window, and looked out, for she could not see it done.

Four sharp quick strokes on each upraised hand, and it was over. Then Daisy was ready to cry ; but Dora's eyes were dry, and flashed angrily into the house-keeper's face. Two or

three quick gasps, were the only signs she gave
that she suffered pain.

" That's enough for to-day, I guess. The next
time will take me longer; but if you're wise
there won't be any next time." With that
parting admonition Mrs. Shote left the room.

Daisy, as soon as the door closed after the
house-keeper, turned from the window, and looked
at her young protege ; she was looking at the
red lines upon her hands, and must have felt
Daisy's gaze upon her, for presently she raised
her head, and flashed her eyes into Daisy's.

In another moment Daisy had both the red,
scarred hands in hers, and was rubbing them
pityingly.

" Poor, poor, hands ! I'm so sorry for them,"
said she, at last. "'I'm so sorry, but what *could*
I do, Dora ? "

" I s'pose I can finish dressing myself, now,
can't I ? " returned Dora, pulling away her hands,
and avoiding Daisy's eyes.

" Certainly," replied Daisy, repelled and disappointed.

" How about locking me up ? "

" You will not be locked up. When you
deserve to be punished again, Mrs. Shote will
attend to you," so saying, Daisy left the room.

CHAPTER V.

LUCY "ROOMS" WITH DORA.

HAT'S the matter with her hair?" said Dora, to Lucy Stone, referring to Anne Porter, half an hour later, as the children were leaving the dining-room.

"I tried to curl it for her, an' it wouldn't curl, then I tried to comb it smooth, an' couldn't, 'cause the bell rang so quick, an' we had to go down. She'll get a black mark, her hair looks so. I'm awful sorry."

" Sorry? "

" Yes; cause she's trying for both prizes."

"Is she, though! It's like her to want both. If I were you I'd rumple her hair up every morning, for her."

"No you wouldn't, 'cause she's promised me if she gets both the dolls she'll let me take one, once in a while."

" How good of her! Why don't you try to

79

get one of the dolls, yourself, if you like it so well as all that?"

"I couldn't get one, I know. I can't remember my lessons if I study ever so hard."

"You might get one for good behavior, for *you* never do anything out of the way, Rolly."

"But I get marks for not looking good."

"Let's look at you! Well, you *do* look as though a cow had . tossed you, that's a fact. I tell you what, Rolly: that old pig Porter musn't get both those prizes. If you'll come into my room every morning, I'll fix you up handsome, see'f I don't; then you'll surely get one of um."

"Oh, will you? But no, it's against the rules for us to go into each other's rooms, to ask for help, when we have a room-mate to help us about anything."

"I'd laugh to see Anne Porter helping you about anything. Did she ever offer to?"

"No, but she's always real good-natured."

"If you think so you must see yourself reflected in her brassy face. Did she have anything to say about cherries, this morning?"

"Oh, Dora, I know all about that. How could you do it?"

"Do what?"

"Get up in the night, an' go off after cherries?"

"How could you get up in the morning, an' eat your breakfast? What's the great difference? She didn't mention that she was much obliged to me for anything, did she?"

"No, but she thought she was sick in the night, an' made me call Mrs. Burns; then she saw the cherry-stones an' told her all about it. She said you would be locked in the study, to-day."

"She must have been so glad, when she said it. Here's Mrs. Burns; I'm going to speak to her," continued Dora, as the teacher entered the school-room, where they now were, to sound the bell that would call all the children to their books.

"Good morning, Mrs. Burns," said Dora, stepping upon the platform, near the teacher's desk.

"Good morning," replied Mrs. Burns, very much surprised, for it was the first time this pupil had ever voluntarily addressed her. "Can I do anything for you?"

"I want to know if Lucy Stone can room with me, instead of Maria Hurd?"

"I don't think a change would be allowed.

6

The probability is, if you should change room-mates, the other children would suddenly dis-cover that they wanted to change, too, which would mix matters up considerably; but I'll speak to Miss Travers about it, and it will be as she says, of course." With that Mrs. Burns turned to speak to another scholar who was standing near her, and Dora passed on towards her seat.

"What are they going to do with you for what you did last night?" said Anne Porter, stopping her, as she passed her desk.

"Do? Why you never saw how they did take on about it."

"It was enough to make them, I should think," replied Anne, curling her upper lip scornfully.

"So I think, but I didn't expect they would be quite so glad."

"Glad?"

"Yes, that there's one girl in school who isn't afraid of her own shadow."

"That sounds likely, doesn't it!" and Anne's lip curled higher. "I don't see why they didn't lock you up."

"Lock me up! Why they've given me the

run of the house, an' I'm to have preserves
every meal, if I want um. I'm to do just as I
want to for two months, an' at the end of that
time I'm to have a hand-organ. Think of that!"

" A hand-*fetter* more like, such as they put on
people's hands when they take them to prison.
What were you saying to Mrs. Burns?"

" I was telling her you'd ought to have a credit
this morning on account of your hair. It's really
very becoming to you, the way it's fixed."

" You needn't trouble yourself about my credits,
I shall have enough of them," and Anne tossed
her head angrily, though she appeared to be
trying to find something that was on a map
hanging on the wall. But Dora wasn't much
interested in maps, and would not take her eyes
from her (Anne's) hair to look at it.

" Lucy says you expect to get both prizes."

" I'm sure I shall get one. I'm the only girl
here that can get a lesson."

" That *does* get a lesson, you mean."

" No, I mean that *can* get one."

" Well you *are* smart, for your kind. I tell
you what, Anne, they promised me a hand-organ,
but didn't say anything about a monkey. Perhaps you'll be good-natured, about that time,

an' won't mind trotting 'round while I grind."
At that moment the bell sounded, and the children took their seats, to begin to study the lessons for the day.

"She hates me, now, worse'n crazy Bet used to hate spiders," said Dora to herself. "I always used to think," continued she, "that I couldn't get a lesson out of a book; now I'm going to try. Wouldn't it be better'n cherries, if I could help Lucy to get one of those prizes. She likes dolls; I don't. But I don't like to be told I *can't* do a thing till I've tried. Everybody told Mrs. Hodges she couldn't stop a hen from setting; but land! she did, by chopping its head off. If I can't get lessons as well as Anne Porter, *my* head ought to be chopped off, true's preaching." With that Dora took out a book, and began to study, much to Mrs. Burns wonder; even the children noticed her unusual conduct, and glanced towards her every once in a while, thinking, perhaps, she was plotting some new mischief.

After the lessons were through for the day, Daisy drove up to the Hall, in the pony phæton as usual, to take the boy and girl who had recited the best, and the boy and girl who had behaved the best, to ride. Dora was standing at the window, when she drove up, but on perceiving her, she immediately left the schoolroom, and went up stairs to her own apartment.

" I think I have a little surprise for you," said Mrs. Burns to Daisy, as the latter entered.

" A surprise ? " repeated Daisy, noticing that Dora was absent, and dreading to hear what would follow.

" Yes, in regard to Dora."

"I don't think it will surprise me much. I'm prepared to hear almost anything about her, always."

" Well, then, I haven't had cause to reprove her once to-day ; and her lessons have been perfect."

" Is that, indeed, true, Mrs. Burns ? " said Daisy, very much surprised, after all.

" Yes, she and Lucy go to ride with you, and little Martin, here, and Edgar."

" Where is she, now ? "

" Perhaps she has gone to her room, to put on her hat. She went out a minute ago."

" You don't know how glad I am to hear that of her, Mrs. Burns. I was beginning to be afraid we could do nothing with her," said Daisy, in a low tone, that the children might not hear. "She is gone long, isn't she? I think I'll go up and speak to her, as the others are ready to go," continued Daisy, immediately proceeding up stairs to Dora's room.

Opening the door softly she looked in. Dora was sitting by the open window, thinking how easy it was, after all, to have perfect lessons, and feeling very well satisfied with herself, indeed.

Don't you want to go to ride, Dora?" said Daisy, as the former turned to see who had opened the door.

"I don't like to ride. Let one of the little ones go in my place," was the reply.

Daisy, disappointed again, turned to leave her, thinking it best to appear perfectly satisfied with her decision, when she was arrested by her saying:

"Has Mrs. Burns said anything about Lucy Stone rooming with me?"

"No."

"She said she would. I want to know if Lucy can room with me, instead of Maria?"

"If Lucy is willing, yes."

"That's all right, then. An' I guess I'll try

for one of the dolls instead of the hand-organ,
if it isn't too late."

" I'm very glad to hear it, and of course it
isn't too late."

" If I should get one I s'pose I can do what
I've a mind to with it, can't I ? "

" Certainly."

" That's all I wanted to know." With that
abrupt dismissal, Dora turned to the window
again, and Daisy, more puzzled than ever, left
her to herself.

An hour after, Lucy came up, with:

" Oh, Dora, how did you do it? "

" Do what? "

" Get me to room with you? You don't know
how glad I am ; an' Anne Porter is furious,
because I said I'd do her work, while she studied
and fixed herself, an' now I'm going to be with
you. She says I'm worse than you are."

" I'm obliged to her. I'd no idea she though
so well of me. She can get Maria to do her
work, that is if she can wake her up in time ;
I think after she tries that a spell, she'll prefer
to do her own work."

" Why wouldn't you go to ride with us?
We had a splendid time. Aunt Daisy talked to

us all the way, an' told us ever so many things we didn't know before. Then we tied the ponies to a tree, an' took a long walk through the woods. An' we found a crow's nest with five young crows in it."

" I would have liked the crows."

" No, you wouldn't. They are homely things, an' most all mouths."

" I don't think they're homely. I had one, once, an' it was so tame it would follow me just like a kitten. I got it out of the nest when it was little, an' had it for months, before anyone found it out, till one day fatty Hodges, Mrs. Hodge's husband, caught it trying to run away with his hammer, to hide it. He tried to kill it, but I managed to get it away, an' I kept it close for a long time, till Mrs. Hodges missed her silver thimble. She said it was silver, though it smelt of brass horridly. Then she said the crow had stolen it, an' hid it away, where no one could ever find it; so she watched me when I went to feed my crow, an' followed me to find out where I kept it, an' when she found out she got her dog, an' set him on it. He killed it. Bit it right through the head."

" Oh, that was too bad!"

" Crazy Bet said she'd go with me an' try to find another crow's nest; but I didn't want another crow; I knew it would get killed like the first. Crow's nests are hard to find. I don' see how you found one to-day."

" Why, we saw the old crow, an' Aunt Daisy said it had a nest somewhere near, she could tell by the way it acted. If we walked in one direction, it would fly at us, an' make a dreadful noise, but if we turned about, an' walked another way it wouldn't notice us; so we walked towards it, till we found the nest. It was on top of a great high tree. Edgar wanted to go up an' look in it, an' Aunt Daisy said he might. Then he brought down one of the young birds for us to see, an' took it back again, after we had seen it. Don't you wish you had been with us ? "

" What do you think of Aunt Daisy, as you call her ? " interrogated Dora, slightly changing the subject.

" What do I think of her ? " repeated Lucy.

" Yes, do you like her ? "

" As though anyone could help liking her, when she's so good. Don't you like her ? "

" I *did* like her."

" Don't you now ? "

"If you keep on asking so many questions, Lucy, you'll know more'n your head can hold. You had better begin to bring your things in here, an' call Maria to take her's out. It'll be supper time in a minute."

Lucy came down the next morning, looking very neat and pretty.

"Oh, I think I understand it now!" said Anne, to herself, on seeing her. "That's all Dora Wentworth's work. She's determined I shan't get both of the prizes, an' as she can't get one herself, she's going to help Lucy to get one, out of spite. I don't care. I'm sure of one, anyhow, if she did have perfect lessons yesterday. She'd have to work pretty hard to catch up with me, after all the time she's lost. I guess I'll keep on trying for both; she'd be so mad if I got them. I wonder where she is? She wasn't down to prayers." But Anne did .not have to wonder long, for at that moment Dora came down, looking as though she had dressed herself in a hurry; but her face was radiant.

"She's been up to more mischief. All the worse for her,"- continued Anne to herself, then aloud, as Dora passed near her, "you have got a mark for not being down to prayers."

" Have I ? " said Dora, innocently.

" Yes; and you'll doubtless have another for not being half dressed."

" That's good. I always did like marks of all kinds. I expect to make my mark, some day, don't I, Mark? " and Dora turned abruptly to a small boy, with a very wide mouth, which was now stretched to its utmost extent; while Anne tossed her head, contemptuously, and walked off. " There, that'll do, Mark. Don't grin any more. You make me think of a box that opens on hinges, an' I feel as though I wanted to take hold of your nose an' open you, when I see your mouth stretched way round like that. Say, Mark, have you got a knife you'll let me take ? "

" A knife ? "

" Yes; a knife."

"I never had a knife in my life."

·" How in the world have you lived so long ? But perhaps you took a dinner-knife, when you wanted to whittle. I've often done that, myself; but I found a splendid three-bladed knife one day in the street. I forgot to bring it with me when I came here, though, an' I never missed

anything so much in my life, as I've missed
that. Have any of the boys got one, do you
know?"

"Don't b'lieve they have. I never saw them
have one."

"Well, if I were you, instead of trying to
win an old toy ship for a prize, I'd speak out,
an' say I'd rather have a 'knife. Twelve boys,
an' not a knife in the crowd!"

"I've got one," said Edgar Ford, who had
heard the conversation between the two, stepping
up, and searching his pockets for the desired
article.

"Let me take it?"

"For how long?"

"A week, perhaps."

"I don't care; only have it handy, in case I
should want it before that time."

"All right."

"Dora?" called Mrs. Burns, who had been
informed by Anne that Dora was borrowing a
knife, and who was made nervous by the knowledge. "Dora?"

"Yes'm."

"What is that you have in your hand?"

"Edgar says it's a knife," replied Dora, opening it. " But I should say it's a screw-driver, seeing the point's gone, an' both edges are alike."

" Is that your knife, Edgar? " said Mrs. B.

" Yes, ma'am."

" Take it back, then. I wouldn't like to trust Dora with a knife. She might get angry with one of the little girls, and do her a harm with it."

" That knife couldn't harm a fly," returned Dora, " but land! you can have it back. I'd as soon try to whittle with the latch of a door as with that," and Dora returned the knife, and walked away, looking very much· disappointed.

Lucy heard the whole and started to follow her. " Dora," said she, taking her by the arm, as she was going out. " Dora, come up to our room a minute."

" What for? "

" I'll tell you when we get there."

" But we can't hear the study-bell there."

" I believe you're trying for a prize, Dora. I saw you studying yesterday as though you were, an' now you're so particular about hearing the study-bell."

" Bother the prize! I'm only trying to see what I can do."

" Well, come up to our room a minute, there is plenty of time. I've got something I want to show you."

" I'm there, then."

A minute later, Lucy was kneeling before the bureau in her room, opening the drawer that held all her earthly possessions. Taking out a small box, she opened it, and took from it something that was carefully wrapt up in paper.

" There ! " said she, handing it to Dora, " you can take that, because you've been so good to me. I'd give it to you, only it used to be my brother's, an' it's all I've got to remember him by."

Dora removed the paper, and exposed to view an ordinary, two-bladed pocket-knife.

" I'm just as glad as I can be ! " exclaimed she, opening the blades to see if they were in a good condition. " It's just what I wanted."

" You won't do any harm with it; will you ? " said Lucy, suddenly remembering what Mrs. Burns had said.

" I won't take it out of this room, Rolly; an' I won't take it at all, if *you* are afraid of me."

" Dear, me ! I wasn't thinking about myself, at all. Tell me what you're going to do with it ? " and Lucy sat down upon the floor, clasping her hands over her knees, and looking inquiringly up into Dora's face.

" I don't mind telling you, if you'll keep still about it. See what I found this morning ! " and Dora drew from under the bed, a block of wood nearly a foot square.

" I don't think that's a very big find," said Lucy, after one glance at it.

" Just look at it. There's not a knot in it, nor a crack."

" What of that? What's it good for, anyhow ? "

" Just you wait, an' you'll see. What kind of an animal does Anne Porter remind you of ? "

" What kind of an animal ? " repeated Lucy, inquiringly, wrinkling up her round face, in a puzzled manner, as she looked at Dora for an explanation.

" Yes ; don't everybody remind you of some kind of an animal? I've found out, at last, what *she's* like ; she's just like the old speckled pig they had at the poor-house, going round sticking her nose into everything, an' trying to get everything for herself. She looks like it, too, about the eyes. Land ! I could almost hear her grunt, this morning, when she was so glad 'cause I got a mark."

" What's that to do with the block ? "

" I'm going to cut a pig out of it, an' write on it, ' a good likeness of Anne Porter.' Then I'll put it in her desk. Won't she be mad when she sees it ! I'll bet she won't eat any pork for a mouth afterwards."

" You can't cut a pig out of that block," said Lucy, incredulously.

" Wait an' see if I can't. I've cut out things before to-day, I guess. If I cut out Mrs. Hodge's face once, I cut it out a dozen times. She always knew it was meant for her face, though I always made it look worse'n she did, a purpose."

" Didn't it make her mad ? "

" I guess so, though I never happened to be 'round when she found it. I used to sly into her room, when she was eatin' dinner, an' put it on the bureau, right front of the looking glass, where she'd see it, first thing, when she went up to comb her hair. Crazy Bet said she thought her husband made it an' put it there, as he used to be whittling 'bout all the time ; an' she'd make him step round lively, for a week

afterwards, every time. But then he'd make *us*
step 'round lively, in turn, so I didn't make
much by it, an' gave up doing it, after a
while."

" We'd better go down, now ! " exclaimed
Lucy, suddenly springing to her feet, as she
thought it must be time for study. And Dora,
after carefully hiding the block and knife under
the bed, followed her to the recitation room,
which they reached not a minute too soon.

That day also, Dora's lessons were perfect,
to the surprise of all but herself. But Anne was
not at all alarmed. She felt quite sure that
Dora could not now catch up with her, even
if she herself did miss occasionally, and rather
enjoyed witnessing her late attempts.

This day as the day before, Dora refused to
take a ride with Daisy, and the latter did not
urge her to go. Lucy lost her ride by some
small misdemeanor ; so after lessons were over,
both the girls went up to their room together,
where Dora pulled out the block, and sitting
down by the window, began to whittle away at
it, while Lucy seated herself on the floor before
her, to watch her proceedings.

" I don't see why you wouldn't take your

7

ride," said Lucy, at last, after watching for ten
minutes and perceiving no signs of a pig in the
block in Dora's hands. " If you don't like Aunt
Daisy, you'd ought to be ashamed of yourself,
after what she's done for you, an' you're the
only one in the school that doesn't think she's
splendid." Dora stopped whittling, and looked
at Lucy, a little surprised at her unusual earnestness.

" Did I say I didn't like her ? "

" You act it plain enough, without saying
it."

" There's no love lost, anyway ; so don't fret
about it, Rolly, you'll lose flesh if you do."

" Then you *don't* like her ? "

" No, I don't, if you must know. I rather
guess I hate her. She isn't much older'n I am,
anyway, an' the idea of her telling Mrs. Shote
to do what she did. If I ever get a chance to
pay her back, I will ; see'f I don't ! "

" Oh, Dora, you wouldn't harm Aunt Daisy ! "
and Lucy's round eyes opened very wide with
amazement.   .

" Can't tell till I get a chance. Guess I'd like
to give her just as good as she gave me, anyhow.
Now see here, Rolly, I don't want to get mad

with you, an' nothing 'll make me unless you keep on talking about Aunt Daisy. The one that made that knife didn't have common sense ! Might'a known such a shaped handle as that would blister anyone's hands," continued she, dropping the knife and block in her lap, and looking at the blister that had come already upon her hand.

Lucy made no reply, but the expression upon her face showed that Dora had fallen greatly in her estimation. Presently she arose and left the room.

" I don't suppose, now," said Dora to herself, as soon as she had gone, winding her handker-chief around the handle of the knife to protect her hand. " I don't suppose now, she'll ever like me again as well as she did. Nobody ever did like me but Crazy Bet, an' perhaps she wouldn't if she hadn't been crazy. I almost wish I was back again with her. I wonder if she misses me, an' if she ever gets any tea, now. Poor, old Bet ! " then, after a pause, " I wasn't sure that I hated Aunt Daisy before, but now I'm sure of it."

CHAPTER VI

DORA " PAYS " DAISY.

"AUNT DAISY."

"Well, Lucy? What is it?" and Daisy took both of Lucy's plump little hands in her own, and smiled down into her round face; for of all the girls at Hive Hall this was her favorite.

"I want to tell you something."

"Well, I'm listening."

"It's about Dora."

"What about her?"

"I want you to be careful, an' not give her a chance to hurt you; because she would, I know, if she should get you alone."

"Oh, Lucy, I'm sorry to hear you talk like that. I thought you and she were going to be great friends, and was very glad of it. What is the trouble between you?"

"There's no trouble, an' we are friends; but

100

she said she'd pay you back for what you did
to her, an' I know she'll keep her word. She
was always real good to me, an' I wouldn't
have told, only I don't want you to get hurt."

" Did she say what it was I did to her?"

" No. You will not do anything to her for
saying what she did, will you? "

" Certainly not. And, Lucy, though it would
have been better if you had tried to reason with
her and convince her that she was wrong,
instead of coming to me and repeating what she
had told you in confidence, and what, perhaps,
she did not mean at all; nevertheless, I am very
glad you did tell me, for it may be the means
of making us understand each other. Now run
along ; there's the supper-bell."

A surprise awaited the children, in the shape
of a treat ; for after they had finished their usual
supper, in came Mrs. Shote with a great basket
of white-heart cherries, and every plate was
heaped high with the delicious fruit, that had
been picked from the very tree on which Dora
had made her midnight raid.

Dora, on seeing them, did not appear so
delighted as the other children did, and seemed
to eat them with reluctance.

"I guess Dora don't like cherries," said one little girl to Anne Porter.

"Why?" said Anne, who knew better.

"'Cause she eats them as though she didn't," was the reply, as the speaker held up two to eat at once.

"Oh, that's because she didn't steal them."

"Steal them?" said the first speaker, loud enough for Dora to hear.

"Yes; wait till we go out, an' I'll tell you all about it."

"I don't want you to ever mention that matter again," said Daisy in a low tone to Anne; she had been standing behind them, and had heard all — then walking over to Dora, who was now eating her cherries with evident satisfaction, she bent down, and putting her face close to Dora's, said:

"I want you to come up to my study as soon as you have finished your cherries; I will only keep you a few minutes," then she went out, and left the children to themselves.

Dora sat until she had finished her last cherry; then she went up to her room, and, pulling out her block from its hiding-place, began to whittle. She worked away at it, diligently, for perhaps ten minutes, looking very ill at ease, and dissatisfied. Presently she arose, and putting back the block and knife, said to herself: " I may as well hear what she's got to say, anyway. She'll bring Mrs. Shote in to me, if I don't, I suppose. I wish I was back with Mrs. Hodges an' crazy Bet — oh, don't I!" With that Dora proceeded towards Daisy's study.

The door was open when she reached it, and Daisy was sitting by the window waiting for her. She arose, as Dora entered, and, going to the door, shut it, and turned the key in the lock.

" I did not do that, Dora, to lock you in," said she, perceiving that Dora noticed the act, " but to lock everybody else out. I asked you to come up here to give you a chance to pay me ; you'll find the same rattan on the desk there, that Mrs. Shote used on you. Why don't you hurry ? " for Dora hesitated. " Is it possible you don't want to pay me, after all ? "

No, it was not possible, for Dora went immediately to the desk, and taking the rattan, approached Daisy with it, trying to look as though everything was just as it should be. Daisy held out her hand. What a tender, little white hand it was! Dora could not help comparing it to her own, which were rough, and coarse, from doing hard work at the poor-house. Well, this hand was tender, and would feel the pain all the more. Down came the rattan relentlessly upon it. Once! twice! three times! Then Dora stole a look into Daisy's face. She stood it bravely. This would decide if she would ever have any power over this girl, and she scarcely felt the pain, her thoughts were so busy imagining how it would end. The fourth time Dora hesitated, but it was only for a moment; down went the rattan again, and with that blow she realized for the first time all that hand had done for her; realized the difference between her life, now, and what it had been before that hand was held out to help her. Up went Daisy's other hand, and down went the rattan upon that, but this time it descended hesitatingly, and Daisy felt no pain; presently she looked into the face before her to see why another blow did not follow, and their eyes met. Then down went the rattan upon the floor, and down went Dora after it, all in a bunch, crying as though her heart would break.

Daisy took up the rattan, and held it towards her, saying:

DORA "PAYS" DAISY. — Page 104.

" You have not finished yet ; there are three more, you know."

" Take it away ! Go away, can't you, an' let me be alone, for a little while," was the broken reply.

" Tell me, first, if we are *even*, now, Dora ? " said Daisy, kneeling down upon the floor beside her. A gasping sob was the only reply.

" Tell me, Dora, are we even, now ? " and Daisy's hand fell softly upon the arm that was trembling with emotion.

" No—no ! oh, go away, till I get over this."

" I'm so sorry we are not, Dora. I'm afraid you'll always hate me."

" What do you want to talk like that, for, when you hate me, you know you do ! " said Dora, hotly, lifting her flushed face.

" *I hate you*, Dora ? You do not believe that, I'm sure. Have I ever given you cause to think that, since you've been here ? " down went Dora's head again, and a low moan was the only reply.

" Tell me, Dora, if you have had cause to think I hate you ? "

" No, no ! but I hate myself ! I hate myself ! I hate myself ! " and Dora snatched Daisy's poor, red hand, that was resting lightly on hers, and pressed it passionately to her wet, hot face.

"You have no cause to do that, either, Dora, for I know that you have a good, loving heart. But you have had a hard time of it, poor child ! and it's no wonder you mistrusted my feeling for you. You will no longer doubt, will you, that I want to be a true friend to you, and you can't tell how much I want you to like me in return," said Daisy, the tears chasing each other down her own cheeks, now.

"I shall always have it to think of—what I did to you, just now."

"It was the very best thing that could have happened, Dora. You might have gone on misunderstanding me for I don't know how long ; and losing your rides, too," continued Daisy, with a little laugh. "You will not refuse to go to ride with me to-morrow, will you? if you earn the right to."

"I never should have refused, only—"

"Only what?" for Dora hesitated to complete her sentence.

"I was sure you hated me, an' wouldn't care to have me with you." Daisy bent down, at that, and pressed upon Dora's forehead the first

kiss she had given her since she had been at
Hive Hall.

" If I had known that—but never mind, you'll
not think it again. Dry your eyes, now, Dora.
They'll be wondering what has become of us,
and they must not see us looking like this,
without an onion to show as the cause," said
Daisy with a laugh, that did not agree with the
expression upon her face. Then thinking that
Dora would regain her composure sooner if alone,
she arose and put on her hat, concealing her
face as much as possible behind her veil; then
taking a book from a stand, she placed it upon
the desk, saying:

"I must go, now, Dora," you can stay here
as long as you want to. Here is a book full
of nice pictures, that you can look at, if you
wish to."

Half an hour later, Dora entered her own
room, "looking kind of queer," so Lucy, who
had been waiting for her, and wondering where
she could be, said to herself, as she entered.

" Where have you been? I thought you were
in a hurry to get that pig done. You'll never
get it done at this rate. I can't see any sign
of a pig yet."

"I guess I won't make a pig," replied Dora, taking the block that Lucy had been looking at.

"There! I knew you'd have to give it up!" and Lucy's face expressed her disappointment.

"What are angels? Lucy."

"Angels? Why don't you know? Angels are in heaven."

"But what are they?"

"Why, everybody that's real good, when they die they go to heaven, an' are angels."

"Do you think it would please a lady, if I should cut an angel out of this block, an' give it to her, an' tell her she'll be an angel sometime?"

"Why, I don't know," replied Lucy, hesitatingly. "That's as much as to say she ain't one now, an' it might make her mad."

"I thought you said they couldn't be angels till they died."

"So they can't; not real angels; but lots of folks think they're angels, an' sometimes, if anyone is very good, they're called angels before they die. Like a woman that used to live in the town I came from; everybody said *she* was an angel."

" Then how would it do to cut out an angel,
an' make it look as much as I can like the one
I'm going to give it to, an' put her name on
it ? "

" She'd like that. But you're not going to
cut an angel out of that block, are you ? "

" Yes."

" That's the greatest ! get a pig half made,
then make it into an angel ! "

" The pig wasn't half made. You don't know
anything about it."

" I know that if the one you give the angel to,
should hear how it was made, she'd think you
meant to tell her she's pig inside, an' angel
out."

" Lucy Stone, do you see anything about that
block that looks like a pig ? " said Dora, her
eyes flashing.

" Not a thing ; I only see a hump."

" It's nothing but a block of wood, is it ? "

" That's all."

" Well, I'm going to make an angel out of
that block of wood, an' don't you dare to say
anything more about a pig."

Anne was not at all satisfied with Maria
Hurd for a room-mate. She was too young to

talk to, and too lazy to be any help at all; so
Anne was resolved that she would have Lucy,
with her good-natured face and willing hands
back again. She felt quite sure that she could
easily induce her to return, for by this time she
was doubtless tired of Dora, and her disagreeable
ways, and would be only too glad to leave her,
if asked to do so.

"She must be getting well punished for going
away," thought Anne, one morning, while standing before the glass, combing her hair. "I think
I'll let her stay there a while longer, so she'll
get enough of it. Then I'll make her think
that I don't care whether she comes back or
not; but if she really wants to she can, I'll tell
her. Then won't she be glad enough to make
the bed every morning, an' sweep out the room
for me. In the meantime," continued Anne to
herself, casting a look at Maria, who was seated
upon the floor tying her shoes, and looking very
sleepy, indeed. "In the meantime perhaps I
can get that girl to do something, by threaten-
ing to send her back to Dora! I never thought
of that," and Anne turned from the glass to try
the experiment.

"Maria?" Maria looked up without speaking, and without stopping the work she was engaged at.

"How would you like to go back to Dora's room?"

"Makes no odds to me where I go." replied Maria, yawning fearfully, and resting her chin on her knee the while.

"Which do you like the best—me or Dora?"

"Don't like neither of you too well."

"It seems as though you might tell which of us you like best, but if you won't then which of us do you think's the smartest?"

"Dora, by a long chalk," replied Maria, arising to her feet and walking towards the door.

"It's a waste of time trying to talk to an idiot," observed Anne, contemptuously, turning to the glass again.

"What's an idiot?" questioned Maria, pausing.

"Look in the glass, an you'll see one."

"I'm looking, but I only see your face!"

"Go down stairs, if you're going! Do you hear?" and Anne stamped smartly upon the floor. Maria opened the door suddenly, looking very much bewildered at the turn affairs had taken, and there stood Dora, and Lucy, laughing to themselves. Anne no sooner saw them, than she slammed the door in their faces, but not before Maria had time to get out.

" See here Maria," said Dora, in a low tone, taking hold of Maria's shoulder. " Just say what you want me to do for you, an' I'll do it, see'f I don't; 'cause you did that well, you know you did."

" Let me alone, can't you ? " said Maria, shrinking away, and frowning. " I ain't done nothing to nobody, an' I just wish folks would let me alone."

" Oh, I'll let you alone, if that's all; but you're too modest. You might have asked more, an' got it."

With that Dora joined Lucy, laughing, and they went down stairs together, leaving Maria to follow at her pleasure.

A week later Anne thought it was time to hint to Lucy that she could room with her again, if she wanted to, and was not a little surprised when Lucy refused to take the hint. But after thinking awhile, she came to the conclusion that Lucy was angry because she had not asked her to return before. " I shan't hint to her again," said she to herself. " She'll have to come to me, now, an' ask me to let her come back : that's all she'll make by it," and Anne thought, with satisfaction, of how reluctantly she would appear to give her consent, when she should ask it of her.

But Anne was never to experience that gratification, for a wonderful friendship had sprung up between the two girls, since Lucy was made aware of Dora's changed feeling for Aunt Daisy ; and the knowledge that the angel, that was now nearly completed was intended for Daisy, kept Lucy in a fever of anxiety for fear it would prove a failure after all.

8

CHAPTER VII.

A SURPRISE FOR "AUNT DAISY."

"THERE, Lucy, it is done!"

"All done? Let me see it now," and Lucy held out her hand to receive the image that was at last completed.

"It don't look so good as I wanted it to," said Dora, with a sigh, "for the old knife got dull, an' I didn't have anything to sharpen it on. But I guess it'll do."

"I think it is splendid! an' it looks ever so much like Aunt Daisy, too; only wasn't it too bad that knot in the wood happened to be there; it nearly spoilt one ear."

"Never mind, it isn't so bad as though it had been on the face."

"I don't see how you could make the wings so well," and Lucy scrutinized first one wing, then the other, while Dora watched her, with a pleased expression upon her face.

114

"Oh, that was easy enough to do," said she, "I remembered just how my old crow's wings looked, you see."

"Are you going to give it to her, to-day?"

"Yes. I wish I had a box, or something to put it in. You don't know of anything, do you? 'cause I don't like to give it to her right out plain."

"You might wrap it up in a paper. I've got a nice white piece that I'll give you, that'll be just the thing," and Lucy went to the bureau where she kept all her treasures, for the paper.

"There she goes, now!" exclaimed Dora, glancing out of the window, and seeing Daisy walking down the road away from Hive Hall. "If we could only give it to her now, it would be better'n giving it where all the children could see it, an' wonder what it is."

"So we can. Here's the paper: hurry up an' do it up, an' run down with it!"

Dora took the paper, and wrapt the image in it, but instead of going down to give it to her, she sat watching her retreating form.

"Why don't you go, if you're going?" said Lucy, giving her an impatient push.

"I guess I won't give it to her, after all, and Dora began to unwrap the paper from the image."

"Not give it to her? Why?"

"'Cause she might think I was making fun of her. The face don't look much better'n those I used to make of Mrs. Hodges, a'purpose to make her mad."

"Dear, me! Give it to me, an' *I'll* give it to her, an' tell her 'tain't half so good as you could have done if the knife hadn't been dull," and before Dora could hinder her, Lucy was down stairs, and out in the street, running towards Daisy, with the image held high above her head, and calling "Aunt Daisy! Aunt Daisy!" at the top of her voice.

Aunt Daisy stopped, at the first call, and waited for the round, waddling figure to come up to her, and presently Lucy stood before her, all out of breath.

"There!" said she as soon as she could speak, putting the image in Daisy's hand. "There's something Dora made for you. She could have made it ever so much better, only the knife got dull," with that, Lucy turned to retrace her steps, without waiting to hear Daisy's opinion of it; and Dora, watching from her window, saw Daisy remove the paper from the image, then walk slowly on.

" She didn't throw it away, anyhow, an' she didn't seem to act as though she was mad; maybe she'll like it, after all. What did she say ? " continued she, aloud, as Lucy entered, all red and hot, from running.

" I didn't stop to hear. I was afraid Mrs. Burns would see me, an' give me a mark, for going away without permission.

" I guess she wouldn't give you a mark for going that little distance, to speak to Aunt Daisy," replied Dora, in a disappointed tone.

" How would she know how far I'd been, if she saw me come running up the street."

" She'd know you wouldn't go very far, without your hat."

" I didn't think of that," replied Lucy, provoked at her own dullness.

" Grandfather Milly," said Daisy, as soon as she reached home, to that old gentleman, who was seated on the piazza trying to create a disturbance between Bruno and puss, by drawing the latters unsheathed claws over Bruno's nose. " Grandfather Milly, do you remember how you laughed when I ventured to say that one of my ·pupils might prove to be a genius, and if properly educated might become famous ! "

"Ha! ha! ha! Don't make me laugh again, Daisy! don't!"

"Then you don't believe that there's one born genius among my twenty-five scholars?"

"You haven't discovered one, have you?" for something in the expression on Daisy's face made him curious.

"*I* should call the one that made that, a genius," and Daisy put the image in grandfather Milly's hand, triumphantly.

"Did one of the children make this?" said he, with an amused smile. "An angel, with wings, and a chignon. Why, I believe it looks something like you, Daisy; and here's your name carved in at the bottom. That's what I call a neat compliment!"

"My name isn't there, is it?" said Daisy, taking the image again. "Sure enough! and I believe it *does* look like me. For a minute Daisy's eyes twinkled merrily; then a mist gathered over them, so that she could scarcely see the image in her hand.

"Which one of them did it; I don't think I could guess, if I were to try?" said grandfather at last, breaking the reverie she had fallen into.

"I know you couldn't guess. Dora did it."

"You don't mean it!"

" The very last one you would have thought of, isn't it ? "

" What are you going to do with her! send her to Italy ? " and Daisy thought the old man looked very much as though he was laughing, now ; but then he was always laughing.

" I'll give the school a holiday, to-morrow and she shall go with me to Boston; and I'll take her through every art gallery I know of. Then I'll buy her a set of sculptor's tools, and see what she'll do with them."

The next morning as the children had begun their studies, in came a servant from Mr. Milly's, with information that Mrs. Burns was to give them a holiday, and that Dora Wentworth was to dress herself in her best, and return with him.

Lucy followed Dora up to their room to assist her in dressing.

" What do you suppose it's for? " questioned Dora, putting on her best dress that Lucy got out for her, and which she had never had occasion to wear before, on a week day.

" Oh, I know what it's for! Aunt Daisy was pleased with the angel, as I knew she'd be, an' is going to take you somewhere to have a good time. I never was so glad in my life!" and unselfish Lucy bustled around, helping Dora.

"I guess I'm glad, too. I feel just as I did one day at the poor-house, when I saw a hen's nest with fifteen eggs in it, then slipped, an' fell in it, an' smashed um all."

"I want you to remember everything you see, an' do, an' have, so you can tell me all about it, as soon as you get back."

"I wish they'd asked you to go, too."

"Dear me! why should they? I couldn't make an angel, like you did, if I should try till the cows came home. There! now you are all ready."

"It doesn't seem strange, at all, for me to be dressed up, lately," remarked Dora, as she viewed herself in the glass, with satisfaction. "I wish crazy Bet could see me now, just to see 'f she'd know me. I know she wouldn't, 'less I spoke."

Down stairs all the children appeared to be delighted, that they were to have a holiday, except Anne, who could not understand why Dora was to go to Mr. Milly's house, dressed in her best. She walked up and down the hall, feeling very disagreeable, till the two girls came down stairs, then, as soon as Dora had gone, she flew to Lucy, to find out what it meant.

" Why in the world did they send for her, Lucy? I should think she was going to be punished for something, only they wouldn't want her dressed up for that."

" I guess Aunt Daisy's going to take her somewhere to have a good time," replied Lucy.

" Take *her* somewhere? Why, she's the worst girl in school."

"I guess not. She hasn't done anything bad for a month, an' you know it," and Lucy's round eyes almost expressed anger, for a moment.

" What of that? I *never* did anything bad."

" I didn't say Aunt Daisy's going to take her 'cause she's been good, did I?"

" Well, what is she going to take her for, then? It always takes you an hour to answer a question."

" I don't think Dora'd like to have me tell you. I'll ask her, an' if she says she doesn't care, I'll tell you all about it, to-night."

" You needn't. If you're so weak that you can't answer a question without asking ' *Dora* ' if you may, you're to be pitied." And Anne walked away, unable to express, in her movements, all the contempt she felt for poor Lucy, who looked after her, wondering why she wasn't as good-natured towards her as she used to be.

About four o'clock that afternoon Dora returned and hurried up to her room with a good-sized bundle under her arm. At a sight of her radiant face, Lucy's became almost as radiant. " I knew you'd have a good time," said she.

" A *good time!* Oh, Rolly, you don't know anything about it ! " replied Dora, throwing her bundle on the bed, and taking off her hat, which Lucy took, and put away, before Dora had a chance to do it herself.

" I know I don't ; but you're going to tell me all about it, you know."

" I wish I could, but I can't."

" Can't ? " and over Lucy's face came a cloud of disappointment.

"No. How could I tell you, so you'd see things as I saw them ? Oh, Rolly ! If you could have seen all the men, an' women, an' children, an' dogs, an' horses, an' everything, all carved out of stone that I saw to-day, you'd just as lives be blind all the rest of your life, I know !"

Lucy looked doubtful.

" An' *angels* ! Rolly ! How I wished I could have had the old thing I made, just long enough to smash it. But that ain't the best of it! Aunt Daisy said maybe, sometime, I'd be able to make as good as any I saw to-day, if I'd try; an' I'm just *agoing* to try, see 'f I don't!"

"Didn't you see anything else? What's in that bundle?" questioned Lucy.

"That's what I'm to try with. Did you ever see anything like those!" and Dora untied the bundle, and held the tools before Lucy's wondering eyes. "I guess I can do a little better with these, than I could with your knife. Ah! Rolly! But if it hadn't been for your knife, I shouldn't have got these, that's certain.

Presently she dropped the set of tools upon the bed, and going to the door, opened it, just in time to see Anne Porter hurrying from it to her own room.

"That Anne Porter has been at the door, listening all this time!" said she, to Lucy, as she closed the door again and returned to the tools. "Well, I guess I can make a pig, now an' I'll make it look like Anne Porter, too! see 'f I don't."

CHAPTER VIII.

T last the long-talked-of day arrived, in which the four prizes were to be awarded to the four most deserving children at Hive Hall.

There were to be no lessons that day, and the prizes would not be given out till afternoon; so the children had ample time to spare, after donning their holiday clothes, in which to discuss among themselves the prizes, and those who would be most likely to receive them.

One of the boys, Edgar Ford, the best scholar among them, was sure of one of the ships, and his face was radiant in consequence, as he walked around, trying not to look impatient.

Anne, too, felt almost sure of receiving a prize, but not *quite sure* as she had felt a month ago. Who would take the prizes for good behaviour none of them could guess, as their con-

124

duct had been, on an average, about the same, excepting Dora; she received more black marks the first month than any of the others received in the whole three.

Never was the sound of the bell so welcome before, as it was when Mrs. Burns rung it at two o'clock, to call all the children to their places in the school-room.

Grandfather Milly had the seat of honor on the platform, and Daisy was flitting here and there, now speaking to this child, now to that, and now to Mrs. Burns, but never in the same place longer than two minutes at a time. While before them all, on the teacher's desk, were the two handsome, perfect ships, and the two large, wax dolls, with their extra dresses packed neatly away, and locked up in the trunk beside each.

After a few words from Daisy, to the scholars, Mrs. Burns proposed to read the names of the three girls that had gained the highest per cent. in their studies; and taking up a paper she read from it first the name of Anne Porter, who had sixty-eight per cent. Anne looked important, then glanced at the dolls and wondered if one wasn't a little better than the other, and hoped she would get the best one;

but she had no time to think more about it, for Mrs. Burns had read the name of Dora Wentworth, who had seventy per. cent. in her studies. "How's that, Anne Porker?" was Dora's inward exclamation, as she stole a side glance at Anne to see what effect the last name had upon her, but Anne had suddenly discovered a long scratch on her desk and was trying to rub it out.

"I rather 'spect neither of us'll get it," continued Dora, to herself, 'cause there's another name to come yet; but, land! it's all the same to me, so long as I'm two ahead of you, Porker. Next time don't tell a body she can't do a thing till she's tried to do it. That's the greatest!" exclaimed she, almost loud enough to be heard, for Mrs. Burns had read the name of Ella Myers, who was a quiet, unobtrusive girl, who had never mentioned that she was trying for a prize, and none of the other girls had ever mistrusted such a thing. In fact, if they had been asked, any day, if Ella Myers had failed that day, they could not have told, so little notice did they take of her, and of what she did.

"Ella Myers," said Mrs. Burns, "has eighty-two per cent. and is entitled to the prize, which

she will please come and receive." Ella walked
up to the teacher's desk, looking very red in
the face, indeed, and received the gaily dressed
doll, with its trunk full of clothes, from Aunt
Daisy. She was about to return to her seat,
when Mr. Milly said: "I make a move that
you all give three cheers for Ella Myers; only,
boys, don't be noisy about it."

The boys were noisy about it, but no one
seemed to mind it much. So were the girls, all
but Anne, whose lips moved, and that was all.

After order was restored, Mrs. Burns proceeded to read the names of the three girls
whose deportment had been the best. Ella
Myers had sixty-five per cent., Anne Porter had
eighty-two, and Lucy Stone had eighty-five.

"Three cheers for Rolly!" shouted Dora,
springing to her feet, as soon as the last name
with its per cent. was read.

"Hush! Dora; all in good time," said Daisy,
who could not help smiling at Dora's impulsive-
ness; while the boys who were about to give
the cheers at her bidding, subsided, with a laugh
among themselves.

Then Lucy went to receive her prize, very
happy indeed; and she was cheered even louder

than Ella had been, because she was more of a favorite, and because the boys knew it was now their turn, and they would not be much longer in doubt as to which among them would receive the ships.

For the first prize Mrs. Burns said she would only read one boy's name, and that was Edgar Ford, who had ninety per cent. All the other boys were so far behind him, she was ashamed to read their names with their per cent. So Edgar went to receive his prize, and was cheered as he deserved to be.

The other prize went to a poor pale-faced boy, who had had the misfortune to lose one leg; and as he hobbled up to receive the ship, his face glowing with pleasure, not one, among them all, had the heart to envy it of him.

After that Daisy told them that three months from that day they would receive four more prizes; and as she could not tell what each one would rather have, she would let those who earn the right to a prize, say what the prize shall be, provided it does not exceed in value ten dollars.

To make the day still more pleasant, and one to be looked forward to, she had provided a basket of luscious great oranges, which she now exposed to view. Then dismissing the children, each was supplied with one, as they passed out.

" Well, Rolly, you got a doll, after all—didn't you? " said Dora to Lucy, as the two went up to their room.

" Oh, Dora, I never expected to get one, and I'm sure I shouldn't have got this, if it hadn't been for you, fixing me up mornings."

" Anne looked blue, didn't she? "

" Yes. It was too bad, wasn't it, that she didn't get one, when she was trying for both? "

" Too bad? Not a bit of it. It served her just right, *I* think, for being so piggish."

" I mean to tell her she can take mine, sometimes, if she wants to, an' will be very careful of it," said Lucy, putting the doll on the bed, and viewing it with pride and satisfaction.

" You *are* going to let her take it?" said Dora, not a little surprised.

" Yes. Wouldn't you? "

" Don't ask me what *I'd* do. But I ll tell you what crazy Bet would say about it if she was here."

" What would she say? "

" Rolly! Rolly! don't cast pearls before swine!''

Lucy looked puzzled, but she did not question her meaning, as a more important matter suddenly occurred to her.

" Wasn't you trying for a prize, too, Dora ? " interrogated she.

" Me ? Don't think it. What I was trying to do, I did. I only wanted to convince Anne Porker that she isn't so much smarter than other people."

" You don't like her at all, do you ? "

" I like her better'n she likes me, to-day. I'm just as sure of that, as I am that that doll's head'll break just about as easy as you can smash an egg."

" Oh dear ! I wouldn't have it break for the world ! " and at the thought, Lucy lifted up the doll, and made a softer bed for it on the pillow, while Dora took out her tools, and began to work."

" What would you want for a prize the next time ? " said she, to Lucy, after a while.

" Dear me ! " exclaimed Lucy, almost dropping the trunk of clothes she had been admiring, in her surprise at the question. " I'm not going to try for another prize. I've got all I want now. I couldn't get one again, neither, I know ; an' if I could I'd feel mean to take

two prizes, when the other girls are trying so
for one."

" Well, if I was going to try for a prize, I'd
try for something that was alive. Such as a
bird, or a dog, or monkey; something that
would know me, an' like me."

" Then I know what you'd better try for."

" What ? "

" A parrot. They're just the funniest birds
you ever saw."

" I've heard of them, but never saw one."
Dora had learned to say them, instead of 'um.

" I saw one, once. He could say almost anything, and could laugh, an' whistle tunes."

" I wonder if they know much?"

" I guess they do. The lady that owned the
one I saw, used to have a woman come every
week to do the washing; an' she always used
to put the parrot in the room with her, so he
could watch her, an' tell if she stopped washing,
and wasted her time ; an' he'd always tell if she
did, then the lady'd get another woman to do
her washing."

" Like as not he'd lie about it, just for the
sake of seeing a new face. But I'd like one,
ever so much."

" I know you would."

" Wouldn't I make it call pig! pig! pig! every time Anne Porker went by."

" Dear me! Dora, you are always thinking of something to make Anne Porter mad! I wish you wouldn't. I don't see how you can. I *hate* to have anyone mad with me."

" Of course you do. That's because you're not like the kind of an animal I'm like. 'Spect I must be like a porcupine, but you are just like a little rabbit, that wouldn't harm anybody, an' only wants to get out of everybody's way; while I'm always in everyones way, an' sure to hurt those I touch."

" You never hurt me," said Lucy, with a laugh.

" Of.course not, 'cause you never gave me a chance. Whoever heard of a porcupine hurting a rabbit. The rabbit knows enough to keep out of the way of such an ugly thing."

" Did I ever keep out of your way? "

" No; an' it's so queer you don't, I believe it's causing my quills to drop out. I'm sure I haven't got so many to hurt with, as I used to have, before I knew you. If I'm with you much longer, who knows but they'll all go."

CHAPTER IX.

PETS.

A YEAR had passed away since the twenty-four pauper children entered Hive Hall, to be provided for, and educated, by Daisy Travers.

Every . three months four prizes had been bestowed on them, and many of the children, in choosing what their prize should be, followed Dora Wentworth's example, and chose pets. Some of the animals chosen by the boys, such as rabbits, and Guinea pigs, multiplied so fast that Daisy thought it best to have a place built for them, instead of having each boy's room defiled by rude boxes containing them. So a building was erected in the yard, half of which was furnished with large, wire cages, to accommodate the boy's pets ; while the other half had a glass roof, and was furnished inside with one wide shelf, which was partitioned off into twelve

133

parts by wire trellis-work, and each girl owned
one of these parts for her own plants, which
she was encouraged to care for to the best of her
ability.

Opposite the flower-shelf, the day our story
opens, hung four canaries which four of the girls
had been fortunate enough to secure as prizes,
while in a corner, chained to a cross-bar, was a
green parrot, that Dora had succeeded in win-
ning. She was delighted with Polly, at first,
and spent hours trying to teach her to talk; but
Polly seemed adverse to talking about anything but
herself. She would say " Polly! Pretty Polly!
Beau-u-u-tiful Polly ! " and " How do you do,
Polly? " but as soon as Dora would try to teach
her the name of Anne Porter, or, as she tried
to make Polly say it, " Anne Porker ! pig ! pig !
pig ! " Polly would scream fearfully, and she
would be glad to desist, though she never quite
gave up the hope of teaching her it, in time.

Anne Porter was standing very near Polly
this day, tending her plants, of which she had
some very fine specimens, when three little girls
entered, and going up to her, one of them said :

" Anne, are you going to try for a prize, this
time ? "

"Of course I am," replied Anne, transferring a trowel-full of earth from a basket to a flower-pot. " I'll have a new dress this time, an' a handsome one, too."

" A dress ? Why, we can have all the dresses we need, without getting one that way."

" All we need, perhaps, but not all we want. I want to dress better than the rest of the girls, and I'm going to, too."

" You might give us a chance to get a prize this time, you've had so many."

" I don't hinder you."

" You know we can't get one if you big girls try. Dora Wentworth, an' Lucy Stone, an' Ella Myers have all said they wouldn't try this time, but would give us small girls a chance."

" More fools they," said Anne, with a laugh. " And I'll stand all the better chance of getting one myself."

" Anne Porter ! " called another small girl, looking in the door-way at that moment; she was doubtless on the errand the others were.

" Anne Porter ! ". Polly, at the sound of that name, dropped a piece of bread she was eating, and held her head on one side, waiting, perhaps, for the sentence to be finished, as Dora always finished it; and when it was not, thinking doubtless, she could do better herself, she suddenly screamed out, " Anne Porker! pig! pig! pig!" then, elated at her success, she uttered a shrill cry, and repeated it all, just as Dora Wentworth entered.

" *You* taught that bird to say that!" exclaimed Anne, white with rage, turning to Dora, as she entered.

" Polly knows a thing or two, without being taught," replied Dora, with a smile that angered Anne all the more.

" What do you mean by that?"

" She know's the right time to say the right thing; or she knows its almost dinner-time! an', as I often give her a little piece of roast pork at dinner-time, 'cause she likes it so, she wants to know if I've got ' any pork, eh? pig, pig, pig,' that's her way of asking for it."

" There's *that* for your knowing bird!" and Anne lifted her trowel suddenly, and threw it at Polly, cutting short what she was about to say into " Anne Pork—" then off she tumbled from her roost, and was held dangling in the air by her chain.

Dora flew to Polly's relief, while Anne, hoping

the bird would die, made good her escape but of doors.

"Polly! Polly! pretty Polly!" said Dora holding up the bird, and trying to undo the chain, at the same time, while the four small girls stood around, and looked on without saying a word, until Dora had freed the parrot, then one of them ventured to ask if she was hurt.

"I guess not much," replied Dora, feeling if there were any broken bones; while Polly turned one eye up to look in her face, and muttered faintly "pretty Polly."

"Yes, you are a pretty Polly, so you are. I'll never doubt it again," said Dora, then she laughed to herself, as she smoothed down the rumpled feathers.

"What are you doing with Polly," said Lucy Stone, coming in at that moment, her round good-natured face all of a glow, as it almost always was.

"I say!" said Dora, addressing the small girls, "will you four run out a little while? Lucy, an' I want to talk together." The four small girls went out willingly enough, looking knowingly at each other the while.

"What is it?" questioned Lucy, as soon as they had gone.

" Oh, the jolliest news ever you heard. You know what I've been trying to teach Polly for so long ? "

" About Anne ? "

" Yes. She said it off to-day, just as well as I could say it myself; right before Anne, too. Wasn't she furious! I tried to convince her that Polly was talking about her dinner, but she wouldn't believe it, which only goes to prove she is a pig, or she wouldn't be so sensitive about it. What do you think she did ? she threw her trowel at Polly, and knocked her off the roost with it. Sweet-tempered, isn't she ? "

" I'm sorry Polly said it," said Lucy, with a very serious face.

" That's like you. After I was nearly a year teaching her to say it, as soon as she does say it, you're sorry."

" I'm sorry for your sake. Don't you remember how you couldn't use your sculptor's tools that Aunt Daisy gave you, for such a long time, because the first thing you carved out with them was a pig, with Anne's name to it, which you put in her desk. Like as not Anne will make a great fuss about what the parrot said, and maybe they'll take it away from you, an' give

it to one of the boys, because you teach it to
say such spiteful things."

" I wouldn't mind that much, if they gave it
to Edgar Ford. He'd enjoy hearing Polly say
it, quite as much as I would," replied Dora,
with a laugh.

" Dora Wentworth; teacher wants to see you!"
said a little girl putting her head in at the door.

" There! I told you so!" exclaimed Lucy,
in a voice of dismay.

"She didn't let grass grow under her feet
that time, that's a fact. Don't turn gray on
my account, Rolly, till I get back; an' keep an
eye on Polly, will you? Some stray pig might
come along, an' eat her; pigs will eat anything,
you know," with that Dora followed the small
messenger to Mrs. Burns the teacher.

Half an hour later she returned.

" Well? " said Lucy, questioningly.

" Well!" replied Dora, ." they're going to
send Polly to Boston, to-morrow, and change
her for a parrot that's not so highly educated.
Anne Porker knows it, an' she's going 'round,
smacking her lips, as though she'd just swal-
lowed a fine mess of swill. Just wait till I
think how I'll be even with her."

" Oh, Dora, I do wish you'd let it drop, where

it is, and not try to be even with her again. Every bit of trouble you have is caused by that —trying to be even with *her.* I don't think she was so much to blame to-day. If it hadn't been for what you taught Polly there wouldn't have been any trouble."

"How did she know Polly meant her. I explained it to her, good-natured enough, but she wouldn't believe me. If I was to blame, why didn't she throw the trowel at me? Then I could have caught it, an' thrown it back at her, for her to catch, an' throw again. We might have played trowel, till, like as not, we became the best of friends. Instead of that she must throw it at Polly, who wasn't a bit to blame, then, thinking she might have hurt her, an' I would tell, she must rush and tell her story first, so as to get all the blame on me. I'll get an ugly, green toad, an' put it in her bed, see'f I don't!. Won't she *squeal* when she lies down on it!"

"If you do, everyone will know you did it, an' you'll only be punished for it."

"I s'pose every one would know I did that," replied Dora, thoughtfully, "but never mind, I'll think of something."

"Dora."

" Well, Rolly, have you thought of something to save me the trouble? That's good of you."

" Do you remember once of calling yourself a porcupine, with quills to hurt every one that came near you? And you said I had caused some of your quills to drop off. How I wish they would all drop off, then you couldn't hurt yourself; for you do hurt yourself more than anyone else, Dora."

" Now you're talking, Rolly. Whoever heard of a porcupine without any quills! I'd want *one* to defend myself with."

" I'll tell you what I've been thinking of, Dora. I'll let you have one quill to defend yourself, if you'll let me pull all the others out," said Lucy, her face radiant with a new idea.

" How'll you go to work to do that ? " interrogated Dora, with a laugh.

" Why, every time you are going to do something that you really ought not to, you know, I'll get you to promise me that you won't do it, an' I'll call that pulling out a quill. Now, if you'll promise not to trouble Anne for what she did to-day, that will be the first one out."

" Pulling that one out would hurt like sixty. I guess you'll have to call that the quill that's going to stay in."

Dora's room, at Hive Hall now presented a different appearance than it did a year ago. Then there was no way of distinguishing it from the sleeping apartments of the other children, now, every available place in it was adorned with some figure or figures carved from wood or plaster, by Dora; while upon the window-seat, where she had just been admiring it, was a nearly completed statuette, which was intended to represent Una and the lion.

This Dora considered her great triumph. She had tried to make it as near like one she had seen in Boston, as possible, and she felt sure she had succeeded well; though a critic would doubtless have said the lion looked more like. a Newfoundland dog, and Una resembled too strongly the wash-woman style of beauty to be interesting. Nevertheless Dora was proud of it, and so was Lucy, her friend and room-mate; and so, also, was Aunt Daisy, who watched Dora's sculptural attempts with interest.

Dora was now standing before the bureau in her room, from the open drawer of which she had just taken a clean linen collar to wear with her best dress; for it was Sunday morning, and she was preparing to go to church.

Every once in a while she would cast a satisfied glance towards Una.

"What are you going to do with it, when it's done?" questioned Lucy, looking over the top of the towel she was rubbing her round face with, and trying to wink and blink out the soap-suds she had got in her eyes. "You'll have to take down Spring, an' put it up there," and Lucy looked at a small bracket in a corner, on which was a wooden figure of a girl very plentifully supplied with flowers.

"I've been thinking I'll give it to Aunt Daisy, she likes it so well; an' I haven't given her anything since I gave her the angel."

"Dear me; I wish I could make something to give her, too."

"Why don't you embroider a handkerchief or something, an' give it to her. I should think you might; you can sew better than any girl in school.

"Don't you say a word, an' I'll do it!" ejaculated Lucy, joyfully. "I've got a bran-new handkerchief of my own, that I can take, an' I can get embroid'ry cotton from Mrs. Burns; she uses lots of it. You're the best girl ever I saw to think of things."

"You like to sew, don't you?"

" Of course I do. I'd rather sew than do anything."

" I don't see how you can like it. The idea of picking away at soft cloth. If it was something hard, now, like wood or stone, there wouldn't be so much wonder. I rather guess Anne Porker won't be at church to-day," continued Dora, with a meaning smile.

" Why do you guess that? This pleasant day, too! Catch her to stay away if she could. Besides, don't you know she's got a new hat? Made it all herself. She asked Aunt Daisy for some ribbon an' roses, then she made just such a hat out of hers, as she saw in a shop window in the village. I tell you it's gay."

" For all that, Lucy, you can take my word for it, she won't be at church to-day, or if she is there, she'll look mad."

" Oh, Dora! you haven't done anything to her, have you, on account of the parrot?" questioned Lucy, her face growing suddenly sober.

" No, I haven't done anything to *her:* though I'm tempted to, everytime I think of poor Polly, and look at the old parrot I've got now, that can't do anything but bark like a poodle dog.

If he'd only grunt like a hog, instead, there'd be some fun in it."

" Then what makes you think she won't be at church ? "

" I dreamed she wouldn't : that's all."

" Oh, that's nothing," returned innocent Lucy re-assured, " I often dream dreams that don't come true, in fact I don't believe I ever dreamed one that *did* come true."

Half way to church Dora stopped short, and stood irresolute.

" What are you stopping for ? " interrogated Lucy, who was walking beside her.

" Una ! I left her on the window-seat, an' the window's open. You don't suppose she'll fall out, do you ? "

" Of course not; how can she ! unless the lion should take a notion to roar, an' frighten her," replied Lucy, with a laugh.

While Dora and Lucy were dressing themselves for church, Anne and her room-mate, Maria Hurd—were going through the same performance.

" I don't believe the people at church, to-day, will think I belong to this school, when they come to see me with my new hat on," said Anne, pinning on a pink bow, and arranging it to suit her.

Maria, who never had much to say, made no reply, and Anne having arranged the bow to her satisfaction, took down from a shelf the box that contained her new hat.

" O ! goodness me ! what's in it !" ejaculated she, after having placed the box on a chair, and removed the cover.

" What *is* in it ?" questioned Maria, with more curiosity than she usually exhibited.

" O, I don't know ! Some dreadful, horrid things ; just look."

" Why, them's young rats !" exclaimed Maria, who had no idea of grammar, on seeing what was in the hat.

" Rats !" screamed Anne.

" Yes. I don't believe they're a week old yet ; see, their eyes ain't open.

"O, goodness me! how could they get in there ?"

" I don't know, I 'spect there must be an old rat in the room, somewhere, an' she made her nest in your hat; like as not she's under the bed or bureau, now. No, she ain't, neither," continued Maria, after a careful search. " 'Spect she must have gone out of the door."

" Oh ! dear, dear ! I'm afraid they v'e spoilt my hat ! What shall I do with the horrid things, they'd ought to be killed."

" Tip them into the box-cover, an' I'll take them up in the attic. There's a nest up there, with four more in it, just like these ; I found it yesterday, an' was going to tell the house-keeper about it, but forgot it. I'll put there these along with them up there, an' tell her to-morrow."

" There they are ! Take them away ! " exclaimed Anne, tossing them into the box-cover, where they immediately began to kick and squirm.

"I'm afraid my handsome new hat is spoilt ! " said Anne, to herself, as soon as Maria had left the room. " There's a great stain on the rib-bon just where it will show. Oh, dear ! I shall have to have more ribbon, an' make it all over again. I can't go to church to-day, that's certain." And tears of vexation gathered in Anne's eyes, as she pulled the trimming off the hat before putting it away.

"It's the curiousest thing ever I saw ! " exclaimed Maria, re-appearing. " Those four young rats I saw up in the attic yesterday are gone, an' I'll bet those that were in your hat are the same ones."

" What ! " ejaculated Anne, sharply, a suspicion of the truth beginning to dawn in her mind. " How could they get in my hat ? "

" Like as not one of the girls found them, an' put them in for fun."

" Well, if that's how they came there, you can just remember its all your fault, Maria Hurd, that my hat is spoilt. You should have killed them when you saw them, or else told Mrs. Shote, so she could have had them killed. Hurry up, an' go to church. I don't want to see you again to-day."

" Served her right if her hat is spoilt ! " muttered Maria to herself, as she went down stairs. " The old cross-patch ! guess she can take care of her rats herself, another time."

Anne remained in her room until every one in the house had gone to church, then, after waiting a while to make sure none would return for anything, she sought Dora's room.

" Did any one ever see such a mess of rubbish ! " said she, to herself, on entering, looking with contempt on Dora's statuettes. " Ah," continued she, to herself, going to the window, and taking up " Una and the Lion," " this is the one I heard her talking about. She's been a long time working on this. How careless of her to leave it on the window-seat, just where the least touch would knock it out and break it. I mean to see just how easy it will fall out." Then placing it where it was before, she gave it a slight push, and watched it as it fell to the ground, where it broke in many pieces.

" There!" said she, as she started to return to her own room. "It's my opinion she'll be longer putting that together, than I'll be fixing my hat."

" Why, Rolly," exclaimed Dora, on her return from church, " you put Una away, didn't you, after all? That was good of you when I forgot it; but it gave me such a start not to see it on the window-seat when I came in."

" Put it away?" repeated Lucy, looking over Dora's shoulder as she entered, her round eyes very round indeed. "I didn't touch it!"

" You didn't? Then that Anne Porker has got it, an' has hid it out of spite; there was no one else to take it, an' it couldn't go without hands. I'll have it again, if it's in her room, as soon as she goes down to dinner; an' I won't mind rumpling up her things much, either."

" Perhaps it fell out of the window, said

Lucy, as she went to the window and looked out. " Oh, Dora, it's down there, all broken to smash ! "

" Don't say so, Rolly ! it's something else you see I threw a lot of plaster out there yesterday ; " but nevertheless Dora went to the window and looked out, to be sure Lucy was wrong. A moment was long enough to convince her she was not; then she drew in her head, and sank down in a chair, without a word.

" I'm so sorry, Dora ! " said Lucy, with tears in her eyes. " If I had only thought to put it away for you ! "

" Never mind, Rolly, you're not to blame. That's my pay for taking it out on Sunday. Aunt Daisy told me never to touch my work on Sunday, an' I never did before."

" It won't take you so long to do another like it, will it ? "

" I'm not going to do another one like it. I couldn't. I shouldn't feel as I did when I was making that."

" You think so now, but in a day or two I know you 'll think differently. Why, this is just like what Anne put in her new hat ! " exclaimed she, stooping down, and picking up an artificial flower. The next moment she could have bit her tongue for saying it.

"So she was in here, an' did it, after all. I thought it was strange it could fall out without help," said Dora, her eyes flashing.

"Oh, no; I don't believe she was in here, and I'm sure she wouldn't do anything so mean as that," said the little peace-maker. "It might have been in the entry, and we might have brought it in on our dresses, you know."

"Humbug! what's the use of saying that when you know better!"

"Have you done anything to her since—since Polly was taken away?"

"Nothing to deserve such mean treatment in return."

"What did you do?"

"I put some young rats in her new hat. I don't believe they hurt it any, an' if they did, it could be easily fixed. It isn't as though it took months to make a hat."

"Oh, Dora, I told you not to have anything more to do with her, but you wouldn't heed me. You always get the worst of it."

"We'll see who gets the worst of it the next time," replied Dora, quite frightening poor Lucy with her earnestness.

CHAPTER X.

A GIPSY FORTUNE-TELLER.

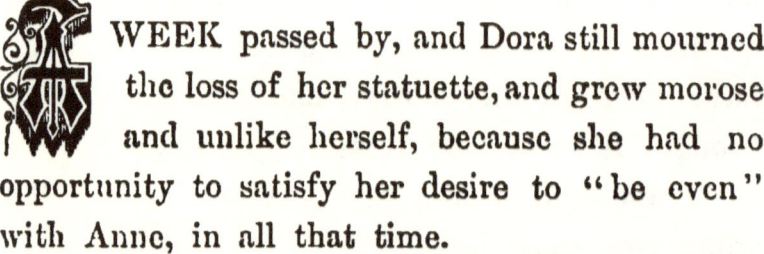WEEK passed by, and Dora still mourned the loss of her statuette, and grew morose and unlike herself, because she had no opportunity to satisfy her desire to "be even" with Anne, in all that time.

Lucy had done her best to discourage her in her design, but all to no purpose. Aunt Daisy was grieved on learning that the statuette was broken, but had no suspicion of the cause of its destruction, for Dora and Lucy had kept the secret so well, that even Anne felt quite sure she was not suspected.

It was Saturday afternoon. Hive Hall was nearly deserted, for all the children but Anne and Dora had gone on a picnic in the woods. Anne had remained behind to trim her hat, and make it even "handsomer than it was before," as she said to herself; while Dora remained

THE GYPSEY FORTUNE-TELLER. — Page 153.

because she knew she would not enjoy herself with the other children, if she went, and preferred to be by herself.

She had wandered about aimlessly, feeling very disagreeable, indeed, the most of the afternoon, and was now standing by the gate, at the entrance of Hive Hall, looking up the way, to catch the first view of the children when they should return.

So busy was she with her thoughts that she did not hear steps approaching in the opposite direction, and could have screamed with fright when a harsh, disagreeable voice close to her ear, said:

" Give me money, money, in my hand, little girl, an' I'll tell your fortune!" Dora, turning quickly, beheld the most repulsive looking gipsy woman she had ever seen. She was large and angular, with a face that expressed wickedness, avarice and cunning.

" I haven't any money!" replied Dora shortly.

" No money! an' live in such a nice house as that! You can get some if you try, I know."

"No I can't. Aunt Daisy never gives us money. She buys everything we need, for us, herself."

" Well, then, if you can't give me money, I'll

take clothes instead. Come, now, I know you've got a dress that you'd give me, for the sake of having your fortune told. A fine fortune yours will be, but I'll not tell a word till you give something."

" I·wouldn't dare to give my dresses away."

" You don't look to be such a coward. Well, then, a pair of shoes would do, or a hat."

" Or a hat!" what a thrill as those words passed through Dora's frame.

" I haven't got any to give away," said she, after a minute's pause." But there's a girl up at the Hall, there, that has just finished a handsome hat, an' you can get it, if you want it."

" Will she give it to me, if I tell her fortune ? "

" No, she wouldn't give it to you, because she thinks too much of it, but you could take it, couldn't you ? " returned Dora, avoiding the gipsy's sharp eyes.

" Ah, I understand," replied the gipsy, with a satisfied chuckle. " She is a bad girl, an' has wronged you ; an' to punish her you want her to lose her hat. That is good! Where shall I find her ? "

Dora looked towards Hive Hall. Mrs. Shote,

the housekeeper was in her own room, seated by the window, sewing. To approach the house by the front way, without being seen by her, would be impossible.

" You will have to go up the drive-way and 'round the house to the back. I will be at the back door to let you in."

" Will there be anybody there ? " said the gipsy, hesitating.

" There is no one in the house but Mrs. Shote, there, an' the girl, who is in another part of the house. You can get out of the way before she can let Mrs. Shote know, if you are smart."

" I'm not afraid of her letting Mrs. Shote know for a while when I'm done with her," replied the gipsy, looking very much gratified, Dora thought.

" You will not harm her ? " said she growing suddenly suspicious. " I will not let you in, unless you promise you will not harm her."

" I won't hurt her. I'll have to gag her, an' tie her, for it wouldn't be well for me to get caught taking her hat ! " with that, the gipsy turned, and walked up the way, with quick, long steps, as though impatient to begin the undertaking. Dora watched her for a moment, feeling not wholly satisfied with what she was about to do, then she walked slowly towards the house, entered, and passed through it to the back door; on opening that, there stood the gipsy on the step.

" I was here before you, after all," said she with a leer.

" You'll have to hurry. The whole school will return in a minute," said Dora, for the gipsy did not seem in a hurry now, but flashed her sharp eyes here and there, in a manner that puzzled Dora exceedingly. Nothing seemed too small for her notice. Even the locks to the doors and windows were scrutinized. After a while her curiosity seemed to be satisfied, and she followed Dora, who ascended the stairs, and designated Anne's room by a gesture ; then after the gipsy entered it, she hurried down stairs again, and stood waiting in the entry for her to return.

Anne had just finished trimming her hat, and was holding it out at arm's length, to admire it, when the gipsy entered.

" Who are you? an' what do you want here? " said she, as soon as her astonishment would allow her to speak.

"I want to tell your fortune, little girl. Give me some money, an' I'll tell it for you," replied the gipsy, going towards her.

"I haven't any money." said Anne, rising from her seat, and moving towards the door.

"No money? well, I'll make something else do, then. Give me that dress, hanging there an' I'll tell it for you," said the gipsy, moving herself towards the door, and placing her hand on the knob.

"That's my best dress. I couldn't give it away if I wanted to, which I don't," replied Anne, decisively.

"That hat that's in your hand, then. I tell you you won't have another chance to know what the future has in store for you; whether you'll be rich or poor, high or low. Ah, I see you've changed your mind, an' will give me the hat."

"No you can't have this hat!" said Anne, putting it behind her, for the gipsy had stretched out her hand to receive it. "But you can have those stockings on the bureau there, if you'll tell it for that."

"Stockings? well sit down in that chair, an' I'll tell it for you," replied the gipsy, taking the stockings, while Anne sat down, feverish with curiosity and expectation.

" You can't have that, too ! " exclaimed she, for the gipsy had taken her skipping-rope from a nail, where it was hanging.

" I sha'n't keep it. I want it but a minute" replied the gipsy, then like a flash the stockings were forced into Anne's mouth, and she, struggling and unable to scream for assistance, was tied hand and foot, then lashed to the chair.

" Your future is soon told," said the gipsy, bending over her with a leer as soon as she was secured." You'll always be unfortunate, but this is one of your worst days ; be thankful it has come, an' will soon be over," with that, she took up the hat that Anne had dropped, then took down the best dress, and with them left the room.

" You didn't hurt her, did you ? " interrogated Dora, pale and uneasy, when the gipsy descended the stairs.

" Bless you bonny eyes, no. Shall I tell your fortune.

" No ; I don't want to hear it. Hurry an' get away from here — that's all I want," and Dora, not noticing the dress, that was rolled up, and tucked away under the gipsy's arm, conducted her to the door through which she had entered, and watched her, until her form disappeared from sight, then she left the house, and walked rapidly down the street to meet the children returning from the picnic.

Dora walked on and on. " Why were they so long coming ? " thought she to herself, and at every step, her fears in regard to Anne increased. What if the gipsy had hurt her? She had listened and had heard not the slightest sound. Surely Anne must have had time to make one outcry, unless she had been taken by surprise and knocked senseless. Perhaps she was lying on her room floor now, insensible ! Perhaps—oh, what a chill came over Dora at the thought and a cold sweat started from every pore—Perhaps she was *dead!*

She quickened her steps into a run, then paused abruptly.

" I won't go any farther," said she to herself. "I'll go back, an' send Mrs. Shote to her room ; maybe I will be too late to help her if she is hurt. Oh, whatever made me do such a wicked thing ! " at that moment a distant shout reached her ears and looking, she beheld the school-children returning. "I may as well wait for them, now," said she. "A few minutes can't make a great difference, either way," and Dora seated herself upon a stone, by the road-side, to await the children's approach, looking anything but happy. Poor girl! she had yet to learn that revenge is not for us; that there is One who knows all our wrongs, great and small, and has promised to repay them.

"Oh, Dora!" exclaimed Lucy, who was one of the first to come up to where Dora was seated. "You don't know what a good time we've had all the afternoon? I wish you had been with us."

"I wish I had, too," replied Dora, soberly, looking into the bright animated face before her.

"Well, you look as though you did, I must say. It's your own fault that you didn't go. I knew you'd be sorry for it."

"It's too late to talk about it now: let's get home as soon as we can."

"What's your hurry? I think its splendid here. Did you ever see such a red sunset."

"Bother the sunset, to-night; the other children will all get home before we do," and Dora arose and walked on.

" You are the strangest girl I ever saw. Some evenings you can't look at the sunset long enough, even when it isn't half as handsome as it is now," said Lucy, as she walked along by her side.

" One can't always feel the same."

" Why didn't you come along to the woods if you wanted to so bad? you would have found us all there; you couldn't have missed us. If I had known you felt so about it, I'd have come back after you."

" For goodness sake, Lucy, don't talk any more about it. I know you would; you're the best girl I ever knew. · I don't care about the picnic. I've got the blues, I guess. I want to get home too—to get some supper."

" Oh, if that's all," replied Lucy, with a laugh, " you'll soon be yourself again."

Dora's steps began to grow slower, as they drew near Hive Hall. She would soon know all now. Maria Hurd, Anne's roommate, was one of the first to enter. Dora watched her as she ascended the stairs to her room, to remove her hat and brush her hair, before appearing at the supper table.

Then Dora entered, and stopped at the foot of

11

the stairs to listen, while the other children brushed by her, on their way to their rooms.

No unusual sounds greeted her listening ears. Presently Maria re-appeared, looking fresh and clean. Dora looked inquiringly into her face, as she descended the stairs, but her face was as expressionless as usual; what could it mean? Dora decided to remain in suspense no longer; she would look into Anne's room herself; but an awful thought suddenly arrested her steps in that direction. What if the gipsy had murdered Anne, and hid the body where Maria could not see it when she entered the room! It must be so, thought Dora, and she bowed her head on the banister in an agony of remorse.

For a while she stood motionless; then, suddenly resolving to know the worst, she ascended the stairs, and opening the door looked into Anne's room; a minute was long enough to prove to her that Anne was not there. Very much puzzled she closed the door, and walked towards her own room; Lucy was just coming out of it, as she approached.

"You look as though you'd seen a ghost, Dora! I never saw you so pale before; are you sick?"

" Sick ? no. What a foolish child you are. Run along down. I'll be down as soon as I brush my hair,'' and Dora entered her room, and shut the door almost in Lucy's sympathizing face. She did not attempt to brush her hair, however, but sank down in a chair, and there remained for she knew not how long.

She, was disturbed at last, by Lucy, who bounced into the room, exclaiming :

" Oh, Dora, have you heard the news ? "

" What news ? " said Dora, starting suddenly.

" About Anne Porter."

" I haven't heard anything about her," Dora managed to articulate. " What about her ? "

" Why you came near losing her, before you got even with her," replied Lucy, with a laugh.

" *Came near* losing her ? " and Dora began to breathe again.

"Yes ; it's the strangest thing ever you heard of. Don't you think, a horrid old gipsy woman, you'd ought to hear Anne describe her, went into her room this afternoon an' wanted to tell her fortune. How I wish I'd been here ; I'd have had mine told." .

" Well, what did she do ? " questioned impatient Dora.

"Anne told her she didn't have any money, then she wanted her best dress, or hat instead, and Anne would not give them to her, of course; so then she took a pair of stockings that were on the bureau, an' forced them into Anne's mouth, so she couldn't cry out, then tied her into a chair, and walked off with the best dress and that unfortunate hat."

"Was Anne hurt?"

"No, not at all; only her jaws are stiff."

"I'm glad!" exclaimed Dora, with a sigh of relief.

"Glad of what?"

"I'm glad she—glad the gipsy took away her best dress, an' that hat."

"Don't be in such a hurry. Aunt Daisy took her to the village and bought her a new hat, the one she saw, and tried to make hers like; then she took her home with her, and gave her a dress; one she used to wear herself, I guess, but I tell you it's gay. Won't she feel big, to-morrow? Why, you'd think she'd done something wonderful, herself, by the way she is putting on airs, and every one is making much of her."

"What do you mean by 'making much of her.'"

" Why, Mrs. Shote took her into her own private room, an' gave her lots of nice things to eat ; then Mrs. Burns took her off to her room, an' I don't know what she gave her, but she came out looking pleased enough; an' Aunt Daisy says she wants her to spend the evening with her, at her house." Dora greeted this information with a low whistle.

" Yes," continued Lucy, with a laugh, " it won't be of any use for us to speak to her for a month, she wouldn't answer us, if we did, she feels so big."

" You forget that I don't speak to her."

" Dear me! so you don't. I don't see how you can help it, at such a time as this, though ; I couldn't. I wish I hadn't gone to the picnic. Perhaps I should be of some consequence, now, if I hadn't. How is it the gipsy didn't touch you, when she got into the house? or wasn't you here ?"

" I was out nearly all the afternoon. Did any of the other girls lose anything ?"

" No ; Mrs. Shote went through all the rooms to see if anything else was stolen. She thinks the gipsy must have got frightened, an' left before she had time to take anything else ?"

" You didn't say who first saw Anne after the gipsy left her? "

" Aunt Daisy. She was going to ride and stopped here, to see if we had left our rooms in good order. When she opened Anne's room door, there was Anne tied in a chair, an' nearly choked to death with the stockings in her mouth. She must have taken on dreadfully about her hat an' dress, for Aunt Daisy took her to the village for a new hat as soon as she had told Mrs. Shote about it all."

" Well, I don't want to hear any more about it. I'm going down to supper."

"Supper? Why, supper was over an hour ago."

" It was? "

" Yes. Wasn't you down to it?"

" It's likely I'd say I was going down to it now if I was."

" Nobody noticed that you wasn't there, we were all having such a talk about Anne and the gipsy. Did you fall asleep? "

" I suppose so," and Dora turned her face to the window.

" Never mind, Dora; I'll go down and tell Mrs. Shote that you fell asleep and didn't hear the supper-bell, an' to give me something for you to eat. It will taste all the nicer, eating it here. I'll tell her I didn't eat anything myself, there was so much talk going on, so she can give enough for two." With that, generous, unsuspecting Lucy left the room.

Dora, as soon as she was alone, began to meditate on how differently the gipsy affair had ended from what she had expected. Anne had certainly gained by it. The only one that lost by it was Aunt Daisy, whom Dora loved more than any one else in the world. The only one that had really suffered by it was herself, while she was in suspense as to Anne's fate.

" Open the door, Dora ! " called Lucy, returning ; and Dora arose to open it, letting in her room-mate who held a waiter on which were two glasses of milk, some sandwiches, and two slices of cake.

" Now won't we have a jolly time all by ourselves. Mrs. Shote was good-natured enough for anything. Just turn that chair around, so I can put this on it; I'm tired of holding it."

" There! you always have to tell me what to do, but you always know just what to do without being told, Rolly," said Dora, as she placed the chair to receive the waiter. "I should have gone to bed hungry, to-night, if it hadn't been for you."

" And I should have gone to bed hungry if it hadn't been for you ; so we're even," replied Lucy with a laugh. "That cake, so Mrs. Shote told me, is some she took out for Anne, but Anne couldn't eat it, she had had so many other things. It's splendid! Full of plums!"

"You eat it all, Rolly ; I don't want any of it " said Dora, pushing it to Lucy's side of the waiter.

" Why not ?" questioned Lucy, her round eyes opening in surprise.

" Because, I don't. There goes Anne Porker," continued she, casting a glance out of the window.

" Yes," replied Lucy, " she's on her way to Aunt Daisy's. How she does swing that new dress of hers, an' isn't that hat a beauty ?"

CHAPTER XI.

POOR DORA.

HAT night Lucy was awakened by hearing Dora moaning and talking in her sleep, as though under the influence of a terrible nightmare.

" Wake up! wake up, Dora !" said she, sitting up in bed, and shaking her suffering companion vigorously. " Wake up, you frighten me."

" I told you not to hurt her! I told you not to hurt her !" mourned Dora.

" Nobody's getting hurt but yourself. Wake up!" and Lucy, with one great effort, pulled Dora into a sitting position.

" What's the matter?" said she, in bewilderment, awake at last.

" I should say what's the matter. You've been having bad dreams."

" It was only a *dream*!" and Dora with a sigh of relief, fell heavily back upon her pillow.

" Only the *nightmare*, you mean. It frightened
me to listen to you. I don't see what made you
have it, when I ate all the cake. What did you
think had got you."

" I don't know," replied Dora, sitting up again
to cast a frightened look around the moon-lit
room.

" I do, then ; you thought that gipsy had got
you; you said as much in your sleep."

" What did I say? " questioned Dora, earnestly.

" I couldn't make out half ; you were scolding
the gipsy, furiously, though, and telling her not
to hurt somebody ; I suppose you meant yourself
by the way you were moaning."

"I suppose so," replied Dora, with another
sigh of relief; then a silence fell between the
two girls which was broken, at last, by Dora.

" Rolly ! "

" What."

" How would you get even with Anne Port—
Porker, if you were in my place ? "

" I wouldn't try to get even with her, at all."

" That's easy for you to say, when she hasn't
done anything to you. But just think if she
should destroy something of yours that you had
been a long time making, and thought a great
deal of, wouldn't you want to get even with her?"

"If I did, like as not she'd destroy something else, to pay me back. That's all the good it would do."

"Oh, well, Rolly, you may say what you have a mind to, but *I* know if she should destroy that handkerchief you are working for Aunt Daisy, you'd be as mad as I was when she threw Una an' the lion out the window."

"I should feel bad to lose the handkerchief, now it's nearly done; but she wouldn't destroy it without cause, I know."

"Do you think she had cause to destroy Una an' the lion?"

"Didn't you put rats in her new hat?"

"I don't think that was cause enough for her to destroy what I had been so long making."

"Perhaps not; but she wouldn't stop to think of that, if she was mad."

"That's right; make it out that I'm the only one to blame, in everything. I believe you're more her friend, now, than you are mine. You had better go an' room with her." To that speech Lucy made no reply. She was pained by it, Dora knew, and she repented of having said it a moment after. "I wonder if I'll always hurt those I do like, an' help those I don't," said she to herself, turning her face to the wall, with a sound that was suspiciously like a sob. Lucy heard it, and one of her plump hands fell on Dora's shoulder caressingly.

"*I* know you didn't mean that, Dora, but I do think you are to blame, for you must see, yourself, if you hadn't put the young rats in her hat, Una would be whole now."

"But my parrot?"

"You would have her now if you hadn't taught her to say what you did. Then you know you made the pig, and put it in Anne's desk, with her name on it, for no cause, whatever."

"It was a good likeness of her, anyway; an' I did it for fun; that was cause enough."

"She didn't like it, if it was for fun; you must have known she wouldn't stand that kind of fun long. I wish you had had your fun with me instead of her, I wouldn't have cared if you had made a dozen pigs, and put my name on them all."

"There wouldn't have been any fun in it unless you cared. What was that noise?"

"I didn't hear anything."

"I did; it sounded as though some one was creeping along in the passage, outside the door." replied Dora, in a whisper.

"Everybody is in bed and asleep long ago," said Lucy, holding her breath to listen.

"There! did you hear it, then?"

"I heard something; what was it?"

"I don't know. What if it should be — robbers!" whispered Dora, sitting up erect.

"Oh, Dora! you'll frighten me to death before morning, I know you will! What would robbers want here?"

"Hush! there it is again!"

"I heard it. Oh, dear me! what are you going to do?"

"I'm going to find out what it is."

"Don't! don't Dora! Lie down an' keep still, can't you?"

"No, I can't. If it's a robber, he is taking off Aunt Daisy's property, an' I won't lie still an' see that done. Let me alone, Rolly, I only want to see what it is."

"But if it *should* be a robber!" whispered Lucy, relaxing her hold on Dora.

"Let's have the sheet! I'll make off I'm a ghost, till I can get in Mrs. Shote's room! She'll know what to do. Hurry!" With that, Dora, impatient at Lucy's slowness in comprehending her, jerked off the sheet. and throwing it over her head, softly approached the d or, and, cautiously opening it, passed out into the passage.

It was quite dark there, save where the moonlight struggled in through the long window at the end; but it was light enough for Dora to see that a robber had evidently been at work there; for the doors, to the long row of closets opposite the sleeping apartments, were open, and the closets, which contained the children's clothing were empty, or nearly so.

" There *has* been a robber here ! " said Dora to herself, " but he's gone, now ; or like as not he's down stairs, this minute, stealing more. I'll wake up Mrs. Shote, as quick as I can." With that Dora hurried along the passage; half way through it, she felt herself suddenly seized from behind ; then, before she had time to articulate a sound, a strong hand was around her throat and a gag forced roughly into her mouth, stretching her jaws apart painfully. Then she was wound up and tied in the sheet she had thrown over her head, and placed noiselessly upon the floor, where she lay powerless to move or cry out, and resembling in form an Egyptian mummy.

Her eyes were free, however, and she made

use of them. She was soon sure that the robber was no other than the gipsy woman she had let into the house that afternoon; and that she had an accomplice was evident, for all the articles stolen had been thrown from the window which was open, to some one outside.

Poor Dora was very miserable while lying there, watching the gipsy, (for that individual had resumed her work as soon as Dora had been disposed of,) and knowing she was now power-less to prevent what would not have hap-pened had not she, herself, opened the way for it.

And Lucy, all alone in bed, awaited Dora's return with feverish anxiety, not understanding why she could still hear that sound as if some one was softly creeping up and down the pas-sage, and not courageous enough to try to discover the cause of it, as Dora had done.

After a while the gipsy, afraid to remain longer, or satisfied with what she had taken, descended the stairs to make her escape out of the house; and Dora, as soon as she had gone, began to roll herself over and over down the passage, until she reached her own door; fortu-nately she had not latched it when she left her apartment, and now, rolling up against it, it flew open, and after a few unsuccessful efforts she managed to roll herself into the room.

Lucy's ear had been quick to catch the strange, muffled sound that Dora made as she rolled along ; her alarm became greater on hearing it, but when it paused before her own door, she sat up in bed, her eyes distended by fright, and fixed upon the door, which soon flew open ; then the awful thing, she could not make out what it was, rolled into the room, and opening her mouth she uttered scream after scream.

Almost simultaneously a voice was heard in the yard below, shouting, " Help ! help ! thieves ! " then the sound of wheels, and of a horse galloping rapidly away, followed, and presently Hive Hall was all ablaze with lights.

It was some time after the gag was removed from Dora's mouth, before she could speak, then she could only say, " The gipsy has stolen everything ! " when she began to cry, as she had never cried before, and no further information could be gained from her. Then Lucy was called upon to explain matters, which she did, to the best of her ability, as soon as she recovered from her astonishment at discovering that the awful thing that rolled into her room was only Dora, after all.

"What is to be done!" said Mrs. Burns to Mrs. Shote, wringing her hands. "The robbers have taken the things off in a wagon, for I heard the sound of wheels; it would be useless to send in pursuit of them, even if there was anyone we could send. What *is* to be done?"

"Who was it that called for help down in the yard?" questioned Mrs. Shote, flashing her eyes around upon the children, who stood huddled together, awe-stricken. "Don't any of you know?" But the children only looked into each other's faces, and replied not.

"I'll run down, and try to discover what it meant." And Mrs. Shote, who could not understand the meaning of the word fear, descended the stairs, and, opening the hall door flashed the rays of the light she was holding into the yard, just as a horse and wagon entered it.

"Whoa, Dobbin!" said the driver, stopping the horse before the door, and throwing the reins over his back. "You're a great deal better on the trot than you look to be, that's a fact!"

"Edgar Ford!" exclaimed Mrs. Shote, nearly dropping her lamp in her surprise at seeing the driver was one of the school-boys. "What does this mean?"

" Don't be in too much of a hurry; help me with these duds, first, then I'll tell you. What in the world do those girls do with so many clothes!" With that, Edgar began to gather up in his arms dress after dress, from the bottom of the wagon, while the children and Mrs. Burns, and the servants came flocking down to see who Mrs. Shote was talking to.

Dora followed the others, thinking perhaps the gipsy had been caught. As soon as her eyes fell upon Edgar, taking the dresses and other articles from the wagon, her face became radiant. "Did you get them all?" called she, hysterically.

" Everything," replied Edgar.

" Not one lost?"

" Not one."

" How did you get them? How did you do it?" questioned many voices.

" Tell me what to do with this horse, first?" said he to Mrs. Shote.

Whose is it?"

"The thieves had it, that's all I know."

" Dear me! dear me!" exclaimed Mrs. Burns, wringing her hands again.

" Can't you tie it in the shed there, till

morning ?" said Mrs. Shote, walking towards the shed, herself, holding her light so he could see, and shielding it from the wind with her hand.

Edgar led the horse after her, and soon had him securely fastened in the open shed; then they both returned to the house, and entered it.

"Now, Edgar, we want you to explain this mysterious affair," said Mrs. Burns, whose patience was almost exhausted.

"It is easy enough to do that," replied Edgar. "I was awake when I heard that team stop by the gate, and I got up and looked out of the window, to see what it was after, at that time of night. I saw two figures get out of it and approach the house, going round to the back door. I watched for them to return, and after a while one came back carrying a large bundle, which he put in the wagon. I couldn't make out what it meant, so I opened the window and slid down to the ground by the lightning-rod, and crept around the house. The entry window upstairs was wide open, and one of the robbers was standing under it, catching the things the other robber threw out to him."

"Sakes alive !" ejaculated Mrs. Shote, lifting her two hands.

"I knew I couldn't get back into the house without letting them see me," continued Edgar, "and it wouldn't do to try to awake you all, for they could easily get away with what they had, before you could get your wits together; so I thought I'd just go 'round to the wagon, and hide near it, till they got in all they intended to take, then when I saw them both coming towards it, I'd jump in myself, and drive off, first shouting loud enough to wake you all up, so the robbers wouldn't think of trying their luck a second time; all of which I did, and here I am, after having had a jolly ride. That horse must understand his business well, for as soon as I got into the team and took up the reins, off he went, as though fifty policemen were after him. He nearly upset me twice while going 'round corners; but I managed to get back without spilling the dry goods."

"You did well, Edgar. I don't see how you could have done better," said Mrs. Burns, after he had ceased speaking. "Aunt Daisy shall hear of your brave conduct, to-morrow. And now, children, you had better return to your beds; you need not fear robbers again to-night. Mrs. Shote will see that the doors and windows are securely fastened."

CHAPTER XII.

CAUGHT IN A STORM.

HE following morning the whole school clustered around Edgar, to hear him tell over again his adventure with the robbers.

Dora would have received as much attention as he, had she been talkative in regard to her encounter with the thief, but she was very reticent concerning it, and all her answers were short and unsatisfactory.

Edgar had just finished speaking, and the children were looking at him in silent admiration, when Dora suddenly broke the silence, by saying :

" Do you want my parrot, Edgar ? "

" Don't I, though ! I'll give you four white mice, and a Guinea pig, if you'll swap," was the reply.

" You can have it for nothing. I don't want

your white mice, or Guinea pig; they're too stupid."

"Then what do you give your parrot away for?"

"I know," said a small boy, looking wise; "it's because you got back her best dress, that the robbers took; she wants to pay you; don't you see?"

"I don't believe that, because Dora doesn't care so much about dresses, as she does about pets, I know. If it was Anne, now, I'd believe you," said Edgar, with a smile.

"It's a pity about 'Anne,'" said that individual, with a toss of her head, and a sneer. "I'd like to know if I ever made such a fuss about a dress, as she made last night on account of hers."

"It wasn't on account of my dress. My jaws ached," said Dora, hotly.

"Mine didn't ache enough to make me cry, an' I was gagged for a longer time than you were."

"Your jaw bones are tougher than mine. I can't help comparing them to the one Samson slew his thousand with, that we were reading about."

" Dora ! " said Mrs. Burns, severely. " That remark was uncalled for, and unladylike."

" And, unfortunately, true," replied Dora, though not loud enough for Mrs. Burns to hear ; then turning to Edgar, she continued : " What was it you said you wanted me to carve out for you, the other day ? "

" You said you wouldn't have time to do it," returned Edgar.

" I shall have plenty of time now, and will do it for you."

" Will you ? That's good of you. I wanted you to carve out a figure-head for my ship."

" I'll do it, if you can tell me what it's to be like."

" I've got a picture of one, that you can go by. I'd like to have it just like the picture, if you can make it."

" Where is the picture ? "

" I'll get it for you." With that Edgar hurried away to his desk, and began a search among papers and books for the picture which he soon found, and returned with it to Dora.

" I can make you one like it," said she, after looking at it a minute. " Don't forget to take your parrot ; you had better get her now, and put her with your other pets."

" Do you really mean it ? "

" Yes."

" All right, then. Much obliged."

" What are they going to do with that horse you took last night ? "

" Why, don't you know about it ? "

" No; I haven't heard any thing."

" The robbers came back again, after we had gone to bed, and took it off; or at least we suppose so, for the horse and team were gone this morning, when I went down to look at them."

" Did they steal any thing that time ? "

" Not a thing. Of course they wouldn't dare to, so soon after getting found out."

" Do you suppose they'll ever come here again ? " questioned Dora, nervously.

" I don't believe they will. If they do Mrs. Shote will see that they don't get in. I heard her say that she was going to have patent locks to all the windows and doors, and wires put up every night, in the entry, so if any one should run against them in the dark, bells will ring."

" I am glad of that."

" I should think you would be. You got the worst of it, last night."

"That's nothing new; I always get the worst of it," replied Dora, as she turned to walk away.

"I don't see what made Dora give away her parrot. I thought she thought every thing of it," said a girl named Emma Goodwin to Anne Porter.

"No doubt she thought every thing of her other parrot, for she had taught it to be as disagreeable as she is, herself," replied Anne, disdainfully. "She can't teach this one what she would like to, so she doesn't want it."

"That must be it. I wonder what made her cry so last night."

"She was frightened nearly out of her wits; which proves she isn't so brave as she'd like to have people believe. I thought it was on account of her dress being stolen, at first, but she hasn't got pride enough to care whether she has a dress or not."

"I don't know about that. I was watching her when she came down stairs to see Edgar, when he came last night. She did look as though she would like to die, till Edgar told us that he had got every thing back from the robbers; then you should have seen how her face changed and she was ready to laugh at anything.

I couldn't help wondering if the change in her was on account of her dress being safe."

" Pshaw! she was getting over her fright, and trying to make us believe she wasn't frightened, after all. *I* can read her like a book."

" Perhaps that was it; though I don't think it was any thing to be ashamed of if she was frightened. Dear me! I know I should have been frightened, if I had been in her place."

" Well, you don't try to make everybody think you are brave, as she does. Don't you remember how she got up in the middle of the night, last summer, and went off after cherries? She didn't care for the cherries. She only wanted to show off."

"Rolly," said Dora, who was talking with Lucy, at the other side of the room. " Just look at Anne Porker! What will you bet she isn't talking about me?"

" What makes you think she is?" said Lucy, glancing at Anne.

" I can tell by her upper lip; it always goes up like that when she's saying something good about me. You see it's hard for her to say any thing good about any one, an' when she does, by accident, I suppose the words burn her lips, as they come through; that's why she sticks her upper lip up so. You'd almost think she was sneering, wouldn't you? but land! she isn't. Let's go up an' ask her what she's saying. Will you?"

"I thought you didn't speak to her at all," replied Lucy, who 'had her own reasons for wishing to keep Dora and Anne apart as much as possible.

"I spoke to her to-day — the first time for a long while; an' I really enjoyed it."

"I don't want you to speak to her again to-day."

"Why not?"

"One reason is because it's Sunday, and if you began to talk with her you might forget that."

"What's the other reason?"

"No good can come of your talking to her, when you two can't agree in any thing."

"Well, Rolly, to please you, I'll agree not to speak to her at all."

"You don't know how glad I am."

"Yes I do; an' I'm going to tell you something that will make you more glad."

"What is it?"

" Last night I resolved that I would never try to get even with her again."

" Oh, Dora! I did not expect to hear that! and I'm so glad, for your sake, because you've been in trouble ever since you began to try to get even with her, I believe."

" You have no idea how much."

"Haven't I? Well, I know enough. How came you to make that good resolve?"

" I happened to think she is such a *mean pig*, if I should get *even* with her, that would make me on a *level* with her, or a mean pig, too. Don't you see?"

"So it would," replied Lucy, with a laugh. " I'm glad you happened to think of that."

" I want two of you, girls, to go to the village for me, on an errand; who will go?" said Mrs. Burns, one oppressively warm afternoon, a few days later.

Instantly a dozen hands were raised.

"I only want two to go; Dora Wentworth and Anne Porter, I think, can go the quickest. You will have to hurry, for it looks as though a thunder-shower is coming up, and I shouldn't want you to get caught in it."

Dora and Anne both were about to decline

going, but thought better of it, for a walk to the village was much to be preferred to spending the afternoon in that hot school-room, studying.

" I needn't speak to her," said Dora to herself. " I'll walk along on the opposite side of the street, as though I didn't know her."

" If she speaks to me, I wont answer her," reflected Anne. " I don't think I'll lose a nice walk to the village just because she's going, too."

Mrs. Burns' motive for choosing Dora and Anne, was, doubtless, because she knew they were not over friendly towards each other, and for that reason would go all the quicker; while two good friends would be likely to talk and loiter by the way.

They had soon received their directions and had started on their way ; Dora immediately crossing to the right of the street, on leaving Hive Hall, much to Anne's satisfaction, for the left side was the shadiest.

As they walked along, Dora watched the black clouds that were rapidly gathering in the heavens, and Anne watched the fashions, on the people she passed. So they reached the village, did their errand, and had started to return, when

Dora felt a large drop of rain on her face. Looking up she saw that the sky was very black, indeed, and that they must hurry if they would escape a wetting. She was about to say as much to Anne, but changed her mind and quickened her steps nearly to a run.

Anne did not need to be told to hurry. She had felt a large drop of rain descend on her best hat, and, after pulling out her handkerchief and covering her hat with it, she quickened her steps also.

" Oh, dear ! " said she to herself, " a mile an' a half farther before we reach Hive Hall. I shall get wet through, I know; there's not a house near to go into. How I wish I hadn't come. I might have known I'd have bad luck, with her for company."

" I can't keep up that trot, from here to Hive Hall," muttered Dora. " I'm in for a wetting, any way, so I might as well take things easy an' enjoy it."

" Anne Porter may as well stop running. Here comes the rain, now ! " and down it came, in torrents, wetting them both through to the skin in a minute.

" Oh, dear me ! dear me ! dear me ! " moaned

Anne, as she still hurried on. Mrs. Burns had
no business to send me on her errands 'when it
looked so much like rain. I'll tell Aunt Daisy
all about her. My new hat is spoilt again, an'
I'm the most unfortunate girl in the world!
Oh!" the last exclamation was caused by a ter-
rific peal of thunder, which followed immediately after a vivid flash of lightning.

"I can't go any farther. I shall be struck
by lightning! I know I shall!" said Anne, in
terror, as another blinding flash and thunder
peal made her pause irresolute.

"That struck near here" said Dore coming
up to where she was standing, awed into for-
getfulness of the animosity between them.

"Oh, what shall I do! I shall be struck, I
know I shall!" and Anne, when another peal
of thunder came, sank to the ground, too frightened to try to go farther.

"Don't do that!" said Dora, taking hold of
her shoulder. "We can get home in less than
half an hour if we try; or there is an old barn
not far from here, that we can stay in till the
storm is over. Come, I say!" and Anne,
scarcely knowing what she did, arose slowly to
her feet and followed Dora, who walked up the

street for a few rods, then turned into a lane, that led to an old forsaken barn; this she entered, and Anne, glad of any shelter, followed her, sinking down upon the floor immediately on entering; her dripping clothes forming a pool around her.

" This is better than being out in the rain, any way," said Dora, " though we couldn't get any wetter if we should try. Like as not we'll have to stay here all night."

"All night!" repeated Anne, after another peal of thunder had spent its fury.

" Yes, unless it clears off, or you cease to be afraid to go on."

" I should die to stay here all night, an' I cannot go on," and Anne wrung some water out of her dress, then put the dress back in the water again, in her excitement.

" I don't believe this will last all night; if it should look like it, an hour from now, I think we had better start on again, for it would be as bad in the end, staying here all night in these wet clothes, as it would to go on, and get struck."

" It's all Mrs. Burns' fault; she had no right to send us when it looked so much like rain."

"She didn't think it would rain so soon; she wouldn't have sent us if she had thought so, I know," replied Dora.

"Oh, dear! dear! it's growing worse and worse!" said Anne, hiding her face in her wet dress to shut out the sight of the lightning, that was now flashing almost incessantly, while the thunder rattled and rolled overhead angrily.

"I've a mind to—" but Dora's sentence was never finished; for at that instant the old barn was struck by lightning, and both the girls were prostrated, insensible.

"The old barn was struck that time. See! it's all afire so quick!" exclaimed a farmer in a blue frock, to a companion, as the two men were hurrying along the street, in the direction of the village.

"Sure enough! They'll see the light at the village, and get the engine out for nothing unless we hurry, an' let them know what's a burning."

"Nothing in it worth saving, is there?"

"Not a thing. I looked in it only this morning, an' it's as empty as a dry well. Come on! with that the two men hurried along, casting now and then a glance behind them at the

13

flames, that were spreading fast over the old
barn, with more curiosity than concern in their
faces, for there was nothing in it worth saving!
Ah! had they only been less sure of that, and
had taken the trouble to look in at the door to
prove the words true, what would have been
their surprise on seeing the two girls lying upon
the floor, unconscious of the flames that were
approaching them nearer every minute.

Five minutes passed away, and Dora opened
her eyes to the flames that were hissing and
leaping before her. For a while she moved not,
thinking it all a dream, till a hot cinder . fell
upon her face, and burned her; then smarting
with pain she sat up, and looked around her.
Where was she! What did it mean! She could
not tell till her eyes rested on Anne's motionless form, then memory returned.

The barn had been struck by lightning! Was
Anne dead? were her first thoughts ; and stag-
gering to her feet she approached her unconscious schoolmate, and all her fright vanished
when she found that she was breathing.

Taking hold of her shoulder, she began to
shake her with a will.

"Come to, can't you? We haven't got ·a

minute to lose! Don't you s e the barn is on fire?" shouted Dora, in her ear; but Anne's eyes would not open.

"There! we can't get out by the door, now," exclaimed Dora, as a part of the frame-work fell, completely closing the door-way. "What can be done! The roof will fall on us in another minute. I could easily get out the window; but it would be dreadful to go an' know she is getting burned up. If I could only lift her up an' throw her out." With that Dora dragged Anne to the window, but all her strength was not enough to enable her to lift the unconscious form to the desired height.

She turned to see how fast the flames were raging, and as she looked a cold sweat started from every pore; then suddenly stooping, she picked up a burning cinder.

"One brought me to my senses — perhaps this will do the same by her," said she, as she pressed it against the palm of Anne's hand. A sigh, and Anne's eyes opened.

"Get up, quick! Don't you see the barn is on fire!" shouted Daisy, shaking her vigorously, and almost before Anne could realize the state of affairs she was out of the window, where she fell to the ground unconscious again.

In a second Dora was out after her, and taking her by the shoulders began to drag her away from the burning building. She was not a minute too soon, for scarcely had she succeeded in getting her a few rods away, when the roof fell in with a crash.

" We are out of that, any way; thanks to a cinder!" said she, to herself, as she paused to look at the burning building. " Now what shall I do?" Shall I leave her here and go to the Hall for help, or stay here with her till she comes to? I guess I'll stay here. With that Dora sat down on the ground beside Anne, to wait until she should regain her senses.

Half an hour passed away, and still there was no sign of returning consciousness; and all that time down poured the rain, and the thunder and lightning raged furiously.

"I wonder what they think has become of us at the Hall," mused she. " They must think we are at the village, with Mrs. Genning. If I had thought she would be so long coming to, I'd have gone for help at first. I've a mind to start, as it is. Maybe she won't come to now before I get back." And after looking once more into the face of unconscious Anne, Dora hurried away.

SAVED FROM THE FLAMES. — Page 196.

CHAPTER XIII.

UNDER ANNE'S WINDOW.

IT was a bright, sunshiny morning ; the air was fresh and cool as it made its way through the open window, into the "sick-room" at Hive Hall, where Anne Porter was lying, watching the birds on the great elm tree, that was so near she could hear the rustling of its leaves, as they were stirred by the wind.

" What restless, dissatisfied things birds are!" thought she to herself, as she watched them, and noticed that not a minute could pass between their coming and going. " What if they had to stay in one place for three weeks as I have had to. But I shan't have to stay here much longer. Aunt Daisy said to-day that I was getting well fast, and would soon be able to go down stairs. She promised me, too, that some of the girls could come in to see me, to-day. Dear, me! I wish some of them would come in now. I

wonder what they've been about all the time
I've been sick." Anne suddenly stopped musing,
for she had caught the sound of a step outside.
" It's one of the girls," said she to herself. " I
wonder which one it is ? " and a flush of pleasure came over her pale face at the thought of
seeing one of her young friends again ; but when
the door opened, and Dora Wentworth entered,
her face expressed nothing but vexation.

" I am glad you are well enough to have visitors, at last," said Dora, approaching the bed,
and holding out her hand, which Anne took no
notice of.

" Where are all the rest of the girls ? It's
very strange they should let you be the first one
to come to see me," said she, petulantly.

" I saw Aunt Daisy before the others did,
and she told · me that you were better. The
other girls will be in as soon as they know it,
and I want to have a little talk with you before
they come."

" I suppose you want to tell me how you
saved my life the day of the storm. Aunt Daisy
told me all about it, so there's no use telling
me again."

" I didn't come to tell you that."

"Perhaps you came in to ask if my hand smarted much. It was like you to burn me like that, when I was unconscious."

"Don't you know why I did it?"

"Of course I know."

"You don't think I did it out of malice, do you," for there was something in Anne's tone that Dora did not like. "That burn was the only thing that saved your life. I couldn't have got you out of the barn if it hadn't been for that."

"Well, then, give the credit to the burn, if it was the only thing that saved my life, and don't take so much to yourself. It was big enough to save my life, that's a fact, and the scar will never go away, I know. I dread seeing the other girls for it will be nothing but 'Dora Wentworth saved your life! Dora Wentworth saved your life!' for a year, at least   I can imagine just how much you've praised yourself up to them, for what you did, or pretended to do."

Dora's eyes flashed angrily, at this ungrateful speech, and a cutting reply nearly escaped her, but she turned abruptly and walked to the window. "I don't believe Rolly, herself, could stand such talk as that, without answering back," soliloquized she. "If Aunt Daisy could have heard her then she wouldn't blame me so much, I guess, if I can't do what she wants me to. I wish I was deaf, just while I'm with her. It must be awful easy for deaf people to keep from quarrelling. But Dora Wentworth, you forget yourself! *you* are a *missionary, she's* a *savage*; you must expect to hear such talk from her." With that Dora lifted her head proudly, and approached the bed again.

"I came to ask your pardon for all the mean things I ever did to you," said she, to Anne.

"Ask my pardon?" repeated Anne, incredulously.

"Yes."

"It's like you to do that, unless you are thinking of something else you are going to do that will put all the rest of your mean acts in the shade," said Anne, suspiciously.

"I'm never going to do another mean act if I can help it, and I think I can. You don't know what the meanest thing was I ever did to you."

"Yes, I do. You put that nest of horrid rats in my best hat. But I got even with you."

" I know you did, and to get even with you in turn, I told that gipsy to steal your hat."

"You did? You told her to steal it?"

" Yes."

" Oh, you mean, bad, wicked girl! Won't I tell Aunt Daisy of that!"

"She knows it already."

" I don't believe it. If she knew it she wouldn't have you here, any longer; she'd send you back to where you came from. I wish she would! I wish she would!"

" But she does know all about it, for I told her myself."

" That sounds likely, doesn't it? You only say that to keep me from telling her. I wish she would come in this minute; but I shall tell her when she does come!"

" Tell her, by all means. You'd never get well unless you did. But I came in to ask your pardon for doing it; have I got it?"

" No, you have *not*!"

" That's all I wanted to know. Of course it's all the same to me, whether I have or not."

With that Dora left the room, and, running down the stairs, seated herself on the chair in the entry, then pulled out her handkercheif to fan herself with.

"Dora Wentworth, you did well!" soliloquized she. "You might have done better, perhaps, if you had been like Aunt Daisy. *She* could have talked it into her in no time, and left her crying great tears of repentance; but I did well by just holding my tongue, when I could have said so much." Dora was so busy fanning herself and soliloquizing, that she did not notice Aunt Daisy's approach until that individual stood beside her.

"I want to hear how it turned out," said she placing a hand on Dora's shoulder, and smiling down into her flushed face.

"It didn't turn out as you would have made it. She's just twice as mad with me as she ever was before."

"And you?"

"I did everything you told me to, as well as I could."

"And she is angry with you now?"

"Yes."

"She forgave you, though, of course."

"No, she didn't."

"Then she is meaner than I took her to be, and your 'mission' will be more difficult than I thought, at first."

" I'm afraid it can't be done by me, Aunt Daisy."

" Discouraged so soon, Dora?"

" I wouldn't be, if I wasn't so much like her myself. It was dreadful hard for me to keep from saying all I wanted to."

" What did you want to say?"

" I wanted to tell her just what I thought of her, in the sharpest words I could think of. I didn't, though, it wouldn't have done her any good if I had."

" No. The only way to do her good is the way I told you. It wouldn't be so hard for you Dora, if you thought less of yourself, and more of her."

" If *you* would only talk to her a little while."

" But I don't intend to. I want *you*, all alone, to do this good work, Dora, as much for your sake, as for hers, remember. Now I will leave you, for here comes Lucy." With that Aunt Daisy turned away, just as Lucy, all out of breath from running, joined Dora, saying :

" What in the world are you doing all alone in this hot entry? Oh, I see! Aunt Daisy has been talking with you."

"Sit down, Rolly. I want to tell you something."

"Sit down *here*, when I'm nearly roasted now! No, I thank you; come out under the elm tree! there's a splendid breeze there, and it's so nice and shady. I've got the funniest book out there, too, that you ever set eyes on."

Without reply, Dora arose to follow Lucy, and they were soon comfortably seated beneath the great elm that grew so near Anne's window.

"Now, what was it you wanted to say?" said Lucy, picking up a book from the grass, that she had been reading, before she went in search of Dora.

"I wanted to tell you about Anne Porter."

It was strange that neither of them noticed that the open window before which a great branch of the tree was dancing, belonged to Anne's room, and Anne herself was near enough to hear every word they said.

"Have you seen her?" questioned Lucy.

"Yes."

"What did you say to her, and she to you. I want to hear all about it, now I'm sure you didn't get in a quarrel."

"We didn't have a very long conversation.

I didn't feel like doing missionary work when I found her such an ungrateful savage."

" Was she ungrateful?"

" I should think so. She didn't even thank me for what I did for her, and she pretends to think that I burned her hand out of malice."

"Oh, Dora, she knows better than that!"

" Then I asked her pardon for all the mean things I had ever done to her, and she wouldn't pardon me!"

" *You did* ask her *pardon?*" exclaimed Lucy, in astonishment.

"Yes! it sounds queer, doesn't it." replied Dora, with a smile.

" I didn't think you would ever do that, and I don't believe I would have done it if I had been in your place. I suppose that quill will grow out again now."

" No it won't. I must expect such things if I'm to be a missionary. I felt mad when I was with her, but I got over it in no time. If there's any such a thing as making her as good a girl as you are, Rolly, I'm going to do it. I promised Aunt Daisy I would." Lucy listened to those words with much satisfaction on her round, good-natured face. Not so, Anne. "Oh," exclaimed she, with an angry jerk at the bed-clothes, "no wonder the girls were no more pleased to know I'm getting well, if that's the way she goes round talking about me. What a hateful, hypocrite she is! I know, now, why she asked my pardon! Trying to make them all think she's a saint! Won't I show her up when I get well! and I *must* get well fast, or there'll be no chance for me."

CHAPTER XIV.

THE READING CLUB.

HE children at Hive Hall, especially the girls, were in a flutter of excitement, for one of their number was soon to leave them, to attend a boarding school, miles away, where he could receive better instruction than good Mrs. Burns could give him; for Aunt Daisy had decided that Edgar Ford must be fitted to enter college, much to his satisfaction, and to the secret satisfaction of most of the boys; for, with his quick understanding, and excellent memory, he gave them no chance to win any of the prizes that were given out for good scholarship.

All the girls, but Dora Wentworth, spent their spare minutes working book-marks and handkerchiefs for him, as parting gifts; Dora was busy carving him an ink-stand that was as original in design as it was amusing, for it was a burlesque on Edgar himself.

It represented a very small boy, with a very large head, who was seated on a pile of books, and many books were scattered about all around him; his chin rested upon his hands, and his elbows upon a large book that was in his lap; upon his face was an exaggerated smile that was supposed to represent contentment. In his head she had ingeniously placed the bottle that was to contain the ink.

"Do you think you can get it done in time to give him before he goes? interrogated Lucy Stone, who was standing beside Dora, as she worked, a few days before Edgar's departure.

"Of course; it's almost done now. Do you think it looks like him?" said Dora, holding the ink-stand out at arm's length for inspection.

"Yes; only it isn't near so good-looking," replied Lucy. "He would like it better if it looked just like him, I know."

"It's likely I'd want him to admire himself every time he dipped his pen in the ink. I made it as bad-looking as I could just to take the conceit out of him."

"Perhaps he'll think you are making fun of him, when he sees it, an' will get mad."

"He's got too much sense for that; he isn't

like Anne Porter. He'll laugh at it, an' like it
better than anything else he gets, perhaps. I
wonder if I can't make his nose look worse,
without spoiling his expression. Think I'll try
it anyway."

"Do you know what Anne made for him?"

"No; what did she?"

"A book-mark with a cat on it, worked in
green silk."

"Ha! ha! she should have worked a pig
instead, then he would have her picture to
remember her by."

"I thought you had given up calling her a
pig, Dora."

"I have, to her face, but to you what's the
odds? You know what she is as well as I do.
Aunt Daisy said I could make her generous and
noble, by being generous and noble myself, in
all my dealings with her. I have done the best
I could, and treated her just as well as I knew
how, ever since she got well, and you know
just how much good it has done. She hates me
worse than she did when I used to do everything I could to plague her. Aunt Daisy was
wrong for once, but I promised her I wouldn't
give up trying to make a saint out of her, so I

can't give it up till I convince her it can't be done."

"What do you think of the reading club?"

"Reading club?" repeated Dora, inquiringly.

"Yes; haven't they said anything to you about it?"

"I haven't heard anything about any reading club."

"I don't see how you could have helped hearing about it, for the girls, and boys, too, are talking about it all the time. Dear me! then you are not a member! That's all Anne Porter's doings, of course."

"You seem to know what you're talking about. I'm thankful for that," said Dora, with a comical look of perplexity.

"The oldest scholars have formed a reading club," explained Lucy. "Aunt Daisy approved of the plan, and she said we could have the hall two evenings out of every week to meet in. We are to read stories and play games, and, Aunt Daisy said she would get Mr. Milly to come often, and play on the violin, while Mrs. Burns plays on the piano for us."

"How long have they been talking about it?" questioned Dora, the expression upon her face proving that she was surprised at the information.

"Nearly a week. They are to have their first meeting to-morrow evening."

"Why didn't you say something to me about it, before?"

"I don't know; unless it was because we talked so much about Edgar's going away, and the ink-stand, I didn't think to mention it. I was sure you knew all about it, too, and would speak to me about it when you felt like it."

"Are you a member?"

"Yes; but I won't be one unless they ask you."

"I don't want you to lose any fun on my account, Rolly. I wonder if Aunt Daisy knows that I'm left out in the cold."

"I don't believe she does. She wouldn't have such actions, I know. She'll make them take you in, if you tell her."

"Then I'll not tell her. It isn't likely I'd want to go to their old club if they don't want me. That accounts for the way the girls have acted for two or three days past; I'd see them talking together fast enough about something, but just as soon as I'd join them, they'd begin

to talk about the weather. I couldn't understand it at all; now it's plain enough. Anne
Porter has succeeded in setting all the girls
against me."

"*All*, Dora?"

"Of course I know she couldn't do anything
with you; and I'm all right so long as the best
girl in school stays by me. How I should enjoy
all this if I wasn't tied by my promise to Aunt
Daisy."

"Enjoy it?"

"Yes. It would be just what I'd like, this
being left out in the cold by such a crowd. I'd
manage to astonish them some way, every time
the club met."

"Aunt Daisy has just come in; I'm going
down to speak to her," said Lucy suddenly turning to leave the room.

"Rolly, stop! don't say anything to her about
their not asking me to join the club."

"That's what I want to speak to her about."

"If you do, Rolly——"

"Well, what if I do? Isn't it better for her
to know it now, than to let her miss you, the
first evening the club meets, then have her send
for you? You'd feel nice, then, wouldn't you,
to have to go in before them all?"

" Do you think she would really send for me, if she didn't see me there? "

" Of course she would."

" Well then, tell her, if you want to, only be sure to add that I wouldn't join the club any way, for the world. If you don't make her believe that, you won't do me a bit of good, Rolly."

Without replying, Lucy left the room to seek Aunt Daisy, who was talking with Mrs. Burns in the school-room. School had been dismissed for some time, and not a scholar was present, much to Lucy's satisfaction, as she entered, and waited for Aunt Daisy to finish her conversation with Mrs. Burns, before speaking to her.

She did not have to wait long. Aunt Daisy's business with the teacher was soon completed, and she approached Lucy with that smile which made it so easy for all the children to go to her with their troubles. After learning that Lucy had something private to communicate, she led her away to her study, where she usually heard all the children's complaints.

Ten minutes later Lucy was with Dora again. " What did she say about it? " questioned the latter, as she entered.

"She wants to see you right away."

"What for?"

"That I don't know. You'll have to tell me when you come back. I'll take care of the ink-stand for you. Hurry! so as not to keep her waiting." With that Lucy took Dora's work from her hands, with an air of authority that proved irresistable.

"I'm going, only don't let anything happen to that; I couldn't make another, you know," cautioned Dora, as she left the room.

Lucy sat down to await her return, with the ink-stand in her hand. It claimed her attention for a while, then she arose and placed it carefully on the bureau, and opening a drawer, took from it her own work, which proved to be a handkerchief, on which she was embroidering the name of Edgar Ford, in fancy letters. She worked at that an hour, then the supper bell rang, and she arose to brush her hair, before going down, just as Dora rushed into the room, her face radiant.

"What did Aunt Daisy say?" questioned Lucy, turning; as she was tying back her hair, to look in Dora's face as she entered.

"Oh, such fun, Rolly, if I can only do it!" was Dora's incomprehensible answer.

" What are you going to try to do ? "

" I can't tell you now. Wait till after supper. I wouldn't tell you then, if I could help myself, because I'm so afraid you'll let it out; for its a dead secret, Rolly."

" A *dead* one? "

" Yes."

" That's all I want to know about it. You can keep it to yourself," replied Lucy, who was just a little offended with Dora, for speaking as though she doubted her ability to keep a secret.

" Oh, but I can't keep it to myself; you have got to be let into it, or else you'd spoil all the fun."

" I'd spoil all the fun? "

" I don't mean intentionally, of course, Rolly. You'd spoil it without meaning to, or knowing what you were doing. But it's no use trying to make you understand until you hear the whole. Won't I have to make sure Anne Porter isn't listening, when I tell you! Are [you ready to go down to supper ? "

" Yes, but you are not. How your hair *does* look."

" Where's the brush ? There! I can't bother any more with it, now," and Dora, after drawing the brush quickly over her hair, once or twice, expressed her readiness to go down stairs.

As the two girls entered the dining-room, Aunt Daisy entered it also through another door. The other children were all in their places, and looked inquiringly at Aunt Daisy, as she entered, for it was something unusual to have her with them at supper-time. Going up to Lucy, she said, in a tone loud enough for all to hear:

" Dora wanted me to tell you, Lucy, that you mustn't think of leaving the reading club on her account. I am very sorry, as all will be, to know that one of the best readers isn't willing to join the club; but we mustn't be selfish. Dora is ambitious to be a great artist one of these days, and she cannot waste her time reading stories and playing games."

" Perhaps she'd join if we should ask her," said Anne Porter, sarcastically, for the benefit of the members of the club.

" Oh, no, indeed she wouldn't," replied Aunt Daisy, pretending not to notice the sarcasm in Anne's voice. " I tried my best to persuade her to, and it's useless to tease her any more. You will lose by it, of course; but, when you consider how much she is gaining, you will not be so selfish as to want her with you, I know."

This speech caused Anne's face to turn red with anger; she wanted to reply, but did not dare to, for fear of seriously offending Aunt Daisy.

Dora took her place at the table, with an air that convinced them all that she knew nothing about their plan of not letting her become a member of the reading club.

"Some one got the start of you, that time, Anne!" said a girl, named Emma Goodwin, as Aunt Daisy left the dining-room, which she did after a few more words to Lucy.

"It will be all the same in the end, no matter which got the start," replied Anne, significantly.

"I don't see how you can make that out," replied Emma.

"What are you talking about?" inquired Dora, looking up with a very innocent expression on her face.

"Nothing much. Why don't you want to join the club?" said Emma, with a sly wink to a girl near her.

"Because it's bad enough to have to read in school, without reading two evenings out of every week; and you know I don't like to play

games.   Nothing would tempt me to join
unless —— "

"Unless what?" questioned two or three girls,
for Dora looked unusually serious.

"Unless you were going to have refreshments."

"Refreshments?"

"Yes; cake and lemonade, for instance, just
before it's through."

"I don't believe Aunt Daisy would let us
have that," said Emma, thoughtfully.

"Neither do I believe she would; that's why
I'd rather be at work in my own room. I'm
going to begin a life-size bust of Aunt Daisy,
next week."

"So you're going to be a great sculptoress,
one of these days," said Mrs. Shote, the house-
keeper, with a broad smile. "You didn't know
that I am a poetess, did you?"

"You a poetess?" exclaimed Dora in surprise,
while all eyes were instantly fixed on the house-
keeper's face.

"Yes. I'll tell you how I came to know it.
I used to keep house once for a family that had
a little girl. Well, that little girl used to be
near crazy about poetry; so one day she comes

to me, an' says she, 'Mrs. Shote, I'm going to be a poetess, when I grow up.' Says I, 'Jennie, can you tell me what poetess means?' She looked mad for a minute, then says she: 'A poetess means one who loves beans,' then she flounced away, but she never said anything more to me about being a poetess, an' I've called myself one ever since, for I am fond of beans· that's a fact." As soon as the laugh that followed the housekeeper's definition of a poetess had subsided, Anne Porter said, sarcastically: "Perhaps our great artist can tell us what sculptoress means."

"Oh, yes," replied Dora, smiling quietly. "A sculptoress is one who can bust anybody's head."

"An elegant definition; but I must say it suits your case, exactly," replied Anne, with a sneer.

"They are usually smart enough to get along without the help of *a porter*! " interposed Lucy, who knew that Dora's tongue was tied by her promise to Aunt Daisy.

"Was anybody speaking to you?" interrogated Anne Porter, angrily. "If you are not more civil you shall not be a member of the reading club."

" Who says so?" questioned Lucy, with a good-natured smile on her round face."

" I do. I am the one that got it up, and I'm president of it."

" It won't be a great while before you are the only member, then," Lucy was about to reply, but Dora's foot came down upon hers with such force, under the table, that the words died away into a low cry of pain, that Anne took for an exclamation of surprise at the information she had just given her, which pacified her, greatly.

" We couldn't get along without Lucy!" said one of the members, to which the others immediately agreed, for she was a general favorite with them all.

Lucy arose from the table without making a reply, and in a few moments the dining-room was quite deserted.

As soon as Dora and Lucy reached their own room, Dora pushed the bed up against the door, then sat down near the window to whisper to Lucy her great secret.

CHAPTER XV.

HE next evening at seven o'clock, the members of the reading club were all assembled in the hall, at Hive Hall, and that room presented a lively appearance. The lamps were all lighted, and Mrs. Burns was playing a sprightly melody on the piano, while some thirty neatly dressed boys and girls [only nine of which belonged to the school, the others being children who resided in the neighborhood,] were talking, and laughing together; for the president had not yet called the club to order.

Presently Aunt Daisy entered, leading a richly dressed girl by the hand.

"This is a little friend of mine, who is visiting me. Don't let her presence interfere with your enjoyment. She can sit on the platform, here, beside Mrs. Burns, where she won't be in anybody's way," explained Aunt Daisy, as she

221

placed a chair near Mrs. Burns, for her young friend.

" Who is she? "   " Did you ever see her before? "   " What's her name? "   "Isn't she dressed to kill? " were some of the whispers that passed around among the children, as they looked at the stranger. While Anne Porter, whose passion for fine clothes was well known, looked on her with admiring eyes.

" Why don't you ask her to join us? " whispered Lucy Stone, to Anne.

"Yes, that's so," said Ella Myers, who had heard Lucy's whisper, as she stood beside Anne. " Nobody wants her sitting up there, staring at us, all the evening."

Anne went immediately up to Aunt Daisy, saying: " We would be pleased to have your friend join us if she would like to."

' This is the president of the club, Anne Porter, Belle Cleverly," said Aunt Daisy, introducing the two. " You heard what Anne said, would you like to join them? "

" Indeed, I should, very much, Miss Porter," replied Belle, to Anne's great delight. It was the first time she had ever been called *Miss* Porter, and to have that title conferred upon

her for the first time by such a handsomely-
dressed young lady, was gratifying, indeed.

"If you will come with me I will introduce
you to some of them," said she, and Belle
immediately pushed her neatly gloved hand
through Anne's arm and walked with her
towards the centre of the hall.

"I'll introduce you to our head boy, first,"
said Anne. "That is the one, at the right. He
is a great scholar, and is going away to a higher
school, to-morrow."

"I don't want to be introduced to him," said
Belle. "I don't like to talk with smart scholars.
I'm always afraid they'll try to find out how
much I know; and, to tell the truth, it's as
much as I can do to tell which came first—
Henry VII or Henry VIII. "Who is that fat,
good-natured looking girl?"

"That is Lucy Stone. I'll introduce you to
her, if you say so."

"Yes. Dear me! I wish you weren't the
president!"

"Why?"

"Because I don't suppose I'll have any chance
to talk with you, you'll have so much to do;
and I'd a great deal rather talk with you, than

with any one else that's here, for it seems to me as though we had known each other for a long while, I really should think you belonged to our school, you dress so much better than any one else that's here."

Anne flushed with pleasure at this flattering remark from Aunt Daisy's gaily-dressed young friend. She *was* better dressed than were the other children at Hive Hall; for, as all the scholars, when they had won a prize for good scholarship or deportment, were allowed to decide what the prize should be, she had always chosen some article of dress, while the others preferred pets, games, toys, etc. She had compared her appearance with theirs, this evening, many times before, but never with so much satisfaction as now; but she had no chance to reply to Belle's remark, for they had stopped before Lucy Stone, who looked at the stranger with something like fright in her round eyes.

"Miss Cleverly, Lucy Stone," pronounced Anne, with an air that would have done credit to a Fifth Avenue belle; it proved too much for Lucy's gravity, however, for her frightened look suddenly vanished, and she greeted Miss Cleverly with a half-suppressed snicker. Anne turned red with anger, but Belle's look of astonishment brought Lucy to her senses.

"I am happy to make your acquaintance," said she, holding out one of her plump, dimpled hands, which Belle merely touched with the tip end of her gloved fingers; then putting her hand again in Anne's arm she walked her away.

"That is an exceedingly ill-bred girl, I should say," said she, as soon as they were out of Lucy's hearing. "She doesn't do Daisy much credit."

"The fact is she has got, for her friend, one of the *worst* girls in school, and, of course, she is learning her ways fast."

"Is that so?"

"Yes."

"Who is the worst girl in school?"

"Her name is Dora Wentworth."

"Can't you point her out to me?"

"Oh, she isn't here. Of course I wouldn't let her become a member of the club."

"Of course not. I didn't think when I spoke. Where is she?"

"Up stairs in her own room, whittling away at an old block of wood."

"Whittling?"   15

" Yes; she would like to make every one believe that she is going to be a great sculptoress, one of these days, so she whittles all the time to convince us."

" I shouldn't think Daisy would let her waste her time so."

" Oh, Aunt Daisy likes to have her ; it keeps her out of mischief, you know."

" So it must. Dear me! I should think you would be tired to death being with such girls. You ought to go to school where I go ; all the girls are perfect ladies, and dress every day as well, if not better, than I am dressed to-night."

" I don't see how you find time to dress so every day," said Anne, looking at Belle's elaborate toilet with a sigh.

" Oh, that's all we have to do. We don't do much studying, I can tell you, unless it is to study the fashions. But they are all looking at you as though they expected you to do something," continued Belle, for Mrs. Burns had stopped playing, and all eyes were fixed on the president, who immediately led Belle to a seat, then stepped upon the platform, and called the meeting to order. Then followed the reading of prose and poetry, and after that Mrs. Burns took her seat at the piano again, which act the children seemed to consider as a signal for them to resume their conversation, which they did, with renewed vigor.

" Which do you think is the best reader ? " said Anne Porter to Belle Cleverly, as she took a seat beside her.

" Your best scholar, by all means. What did you say his name was ? "

" Edgar Ford ? "

" Yes ; he's the best reader I ever heard, if he does belong to this school."

Anne looked towards Edgar, and was silent. She had asked the question hoping to hear her own name mentioned, for she had done her best to read effectively ; however she soon consoled herself with the thought that Belle was no scholar, and so could not be capable of judging correctly.

" What a queer voice that Belle Cleverly has got," said a tall, thin girl to Lucy.

" What's the matter with her voice ? " interrogated Lucy.

" It sounds to me as though she had something in her mouth. She doesn't seem to want to get acquainted, much, after all."

" The way I acted discouraged her from being introduced to any one else, I suppose. I wish I didn't have to laugh just when I ought not to," said Lucy, her face almost serious.

" What made you laugh, then ? "

" The way Anne introduced us. I never saw such airs as she did put on."

" She'll be likely to put on airs after this, since Aunt Daisy's friend has taken such a liking to her. Whom does she remind you of?"

" Who do you mean ? " Miss Cleverly ? "

" Yes."

" I don't know. Does she remind you of any one ? "

" Yes ; she looks like Dora Wentworth to me."

" I should think she did; with that low forehead, and white face! She isn't half so good looking as Dora, I think."

" I think she's better looking ; but it's too bad she's got such a dreadfully queer voice. It makes me nervous to hear her talk."

" I didn't notice anything out of the way about it."

" You must be deaf, then. There, the president has left her! Why don't you go up and speak to her? You are the only one that has been introduced."

"I'd be afraid she wouldn't answer me."

"I would want to, if I were you, just to prove that you have some manners, if nothing else."

"Very well, then; I'll go and speak to her, and I shan't grow gray if she doesn't answer me." With that Lucy walked over toward the stranger, and took the seat beside her that Anne had just vacated.

Anne who had gone to speak with Aunt Daisy about starting some games, was gratified to see that Lucy was treated in a cool or indifferent manner by the fashionable Belle, and as soon as possible she returned to her side, preferring her company to joining in the game.

"Are you going to make Aunt Daisy a long visit!" said she as she returned to Belle.

"I shall stay till after Christmas."

"That will be nearly a month."

"Yes."

"I wish the girls here were more like the girls that go to your school; then you would enjoy coming to our club every time it meets."

"I should enjoy it, as it is. I like to watch them, and hear them read; and if I do not interfere with your duties as president, I should be glad to come every time."

"Of course you do not interfere with my duties as president. What I have to do is easily done."

"Aren't you going to join in the game with your stylish friends?" said Belle, with a deprecating smile.

"Oh, no; I do not care to play," replied Anne, who had always enjoyed having her share in a game before.

"I shouldn't think you would, they are so rude." Then pulling out the handsomest little gold watch Anne had ever seen, she looked at it carelessly, and continued: "Half past eight. Daisy said she was going home at that time, because Mr. Milly isn't very well. I shall have to say good-by," and rising, she held a gloved hand for Anne to shake.

"I shall look for you at our next meeting."

"I shall be here if nothing happens."

Ten minutes afterwards, as Anne was sitting all alone, watching her companions, and thinking of the new acquaintance she had made, a girl came up to her, saying:

"Come, Anne, we want just one more to play this game."

"I don't want to play. I detest such childish games."

"You played it only yesterday, you know you did!"

"Well, I played it then to please you. You can't expect me to do it every day."

"Won't she come?" questioned the waiting children, as their companion returned.

"No;" replied the girl, she says she detests such childish games, and her pug nose went up half an inch higher."

"Nice president she is, I don't think," exclaimed a boy in disgust.

"Let's send for Dora, just to plague her," said Ella Meyers.

"Dora wouldn't come down, I know," said Lucy quickly. "She's just as busy as she can be."

"Then we'll have to play something else," said Edgar Ford, but Mrs. Burns came to the rescue, and proved that she did not detest childish games, by taking the vacant place herself, so good-naturedly, that the children enjoyed it more than they would have done, had Anne joined them instead.

The next morning, at an early hour, Mr. Milly's carriage stopped at Hive Hall, to take Edgar and his baggage to the depot.

He had been greatly surprised, after breakfast, by the number of gifts he had received from the girls. He counted eighteen book-marks, fourteen handkerchiefs, and something that he had been told were slippers, but what earthly good they were, he could not see, as there were no soles to them. He was about to put all those articles in his trunk, when Dora approached him with a paste-board box in her hand, that was securely tied up. This she offered to him, saying it was a parting gift from her.

Edgar looked at the box suspiciously for a moment, then with a knowing smile, shook his head.

" What! won't you take it?" said Dora, incredulously.

" Let's see what's in it first."

" No, sir! it mustn't be opened until you arrive at school."

" If I didn't know you pretty well, Dora, I might take it; then I'd wish I hadn't, when I opened it, and found it full of ground worms, or something equally interesting."

"Edgar Ford!"

"Exactly."

"Do you really think I'd do anything so mean as that?"

"Perhaps you don't remember what you had on the Christmas tree for me last year, a good-looking box enough, full of soap."

"Well, soap is a good thing, isn't it?"

"But it was soft-soap, remember. I was called by that name so long, I don't care to get a new one, thank you."

"Honestly and truly, this is nothing of the kind; and if you don't take it you'll be sorry, that's all, for I'll just show it to you then burn it up; see if I don't." Dora's manner was so earnest, that Edgar was partly convinced; and he took the box, reluctantly.

"Will it break if it drops?" said he.

"Yes; so be careful of it."

"Then it's bad eggs that's in it."

"Give it back to me, if you think so."

"No, I won't, but I'll make sure no one is around when I open it."

"You can do that, and welcome. Now let me see you put it in your trunk."

"They were standing in the entry where his

trunk had been taken, and Edgar immediately stooped down and unlocked it, then packed away the book-marks, handkerchiefs, slippers, and the box from Dora.

" You will write and let me know how you like it, won't you? " said she, with a satisfied smile, after the trunk had been locked again.

" Oh, yes, of course."

" Good-by, then, for here is the carriage," and at that moment the carriage stopped at the door. Aunt Daisy was in it, for she was going to accompany Edgar as far as. the depot, to give him some parting words of good advice.

Edgar assisted the driver to strap his trunk to the back of the carriage, then, entering it, he was driven away, with the sound of many "good-bys" ringing in his ears, from the children who had assembled to see him off.

" What was in that box that Dora Wentworth gave him? " said Anne Porter to Lucy, as soon as the carriage was out of sight.

" A present," replied Lucy.

" I supposed it was; but can't you tell me what kind of a present! "

" The handsomest one he had from us, I think."

" Your opinion isn't worth much," replied
Anne, sarcastically, as she turned to walk away.
She would have given much to know what the
box contained, but it would never do to let
Dora learn that she was at all interested in any
thing she did.

" What did she say was in the box ? " questioned Maria Hurd, [who had heard what Anne
said, but not Lucy's answer,] as Anne
approached her.

" She didn't say. Soft soap, very likely. You
couldn't expect it would be much, from her.
He was foolish to take it."

" He is going to write to her, and let her
know how he likes it, whatever it is."

" He is ? "

" Yes, I heard him say so, just before he
went. But I think I know what's in the box."

" What ? "

" She bought some oranges down town, yesterday, and when she saw I saw them, she said
she would give me one, only she had bought
them for somebody, and there were scarcely
enough to give, as it was."

" That is it, then. Strange I didn't think of
it before ! She pretended that those oranges

were for Mrs. Johnson's little girl, who is sick. Didn't I tell you she was a mean hypocrite? That was done to make Aunt Daisy think she's awfully good, to spend her money for poor sick girls; don't you see?"

"Did she tell you that she bought them for Mrs. Johnson's girl?"

"She didn't; Lucy did. Lucy is getting to be just as bad as she is. I never was so mortified in my life, as I was when I introduced Miss Cleverly to her last evening. It's a wonder she took such a liking to me as she did, when she saw what kind of girls I'm obliged to associate with," and Anne bestowed a contemptuous glance at Dora and Lucy, who were approaching, arm in arm, and talking away as though they had just met after a long separation, and there was lots of news to tell on both sides.

"I say, Dora! won't you tell me what you gave Edgar for a present?" said Ella Meyers, who came after them, and placed her hand on Dora's shoulder.

"Certainly: a caricatural receptacle for writing fluid," replied Dora with a laugh.

"What's that?" said Ella, looking puzzled.

"I'll tell you," interposed Anne, scornfully.

" Those oranges that we all supposed were intended for Edith Johnson, was Dora's present to Edgar."

" Who told you so ? " said Dora.

" Miss Cleverly, I guess," said Lucy, with a laugh.

" Never mind who told me. I know it, and that's enough ; and I want the other girls to know it, too, so they won't have a doubt about your being just what I told them you were."

" What did you tell them I was ? "

" A mean hypocrite."

" Dora's face turned red with anger, and she would have forgotten all about her promise to Aunt Daisy, had not Lucy, her good angel at all times, pressed her arm warningly, and tried to pull her away.

" I don't see why you should work so hard to turn all the girls against me," said she, calmly, after a struggle with her temper, in which she was victorious. " It's a queer way of showing your gratitude to me for saving your life, I must say.

" There it is again ! I wonder how many more times I've got to be reminded of what, perhaps, you never did. It's easy enough for you to say you saved my life, when there was no one near to prove you didn't, and I was unconscious."

" Do you think you would have got out of the burning barn if it hadn't been for me? "

" I am not sure that I was ever in it. I was frightened by the thunder and lightning, I know: but whether I was outside or inside the barn when I fainted away, I have only your word to prove."

" Then you are not ungrateful — only forgetful," said Dora, who could not help speaking sarcastically.

At that moment the recitation bell was heard, which put an end to the altercation.

After school Ella Meyers, who wanted to make sure that Dora's present to Edgar had been oranges, said to Anne :

" Will you come with me to Mrs. Johnson's ? "

" What for? " said Anne, twisting her head around, to see that her dress was fashionably arranged behind.

" To see Sarah."

" No; I don't care about seeing her."

" Do come! I want to find out if Dora was there yesterday."

"Oh!" said Anne, who began to compre-
hend Ella's motive for going. She would not
have hesitated a moment had she been quite
sure that Dora had not given Sarah the oranges;
as it was she said, doubtingly: " But it's such
a horrid place to go to! Mrs. Johnson is always
washing, and the smell of soap-suds is strong
enough to scent one through for a week."

"Well, if you won't go with me, Maria will,"
and Ella turned away to go in search of the
girl she had named.

"I'll go, then, if you want me to," said
Anne, jerking out the words as though she was
somewhat provoked.

CHAPTER XVI

RS. JOHNSON lived half a mile beyond Hive Hall, in a little tumble-down red house, that could boast of a piazza in front, on which — as Anne and Ella approached it — a thin old cat and four kittens were sleeping, all unconscious that their mistress was a very poor woman, who could scarcely spare the saucers of milk they received every morning and night; and that often, while they were enjoying it, she had seriously thought of tying them all up in a bag together with a stone for company, and dropping them in the pond that was so conveniently near the back of the house.

"Scat!" exclaimed Anne, who disliked all kinds of pets, giving them a quick push with her foot, which caused Puss and her four young ones to roll off the piazza step, before they had time to open their eyes. Puss soon picked herself up and walked away, whisking her tail angrily; but the kittens lay just where they had fallen, too astonished to move for some time.

At Ella's knock Mrs. Johnson opened the door. She was a small thin-faced woman, whose skin looked as though it had been intended for a larger person, it hung so loosely, and showed so many wrinkles.

"Is Sarah better to-day?" interrogated Ella, as soon as the door was opened.

"Won't you walk in and see her? She never will be any better in this world," said Mrs. Johnson, with a weary sigh, holding the door open wide for the two girls to pass in; then she conducted them along a narrow passage to the kitchen, where Sarah, her only child, was lying upon the lounge, in the last stages of consumption.

Her face brightened up, as the two girls entered, but it immediately grew dull and lifeless again when she saw who her visitors were. She had doubtless been expecting some one else.

"How do you do Sarah?" said Ella, going towards her, and offering her hand, while her eyes sought the stand, near the lounge, on

16

which were two glasses containing medicine, and three oranges on a plate.

Sarah took the extended hand, but made no reply.

"She doesn't like to talk much, it sets her a coughing," apologized her mother, as she thrust her arms into a wash-tub after some clothes, that she immediately began to rub. Anne then approached the sick girl, and offered her hand without speaking; and a shiver passed through her frame as the thin white fingers closed around her own.

Sarah then opened her lips and said something.

"What did she say?" questioned Anne, of Ella.

"She wants to know if Dora is coming," interposed Mrs. Johnson, "Dora Wentworth, from your school. She comes nearly every day and reads to her; an' her visits do her more good than the medicine, I think."

"Was she here yesterday?" said Ella with a look in Anne's face.

"Indeed she was, an' brought her those nice oranges. You mustn't expect she can come every day, Sarah." Sarah was not satisfied with that reply from her mother, but looked inquiringly into Anne's face.

" I couldn't tell you whether she's coming or not," said Anne, in reply to the look.

" If you will get me a book, I will read to her," said Ella, addressing Mrs. Johnson.

" Dear! dear! where could the likes of me get books? Dora always brings a book with her."

" Then it's of no use for us to stay longer," said Anne, " as it hurts her to talk, and we have nothing to read to her."

" I hope you'll be better the next time I come ; for I'm coming again, and the next time I'll not come empty-handed," said Ella, taking the wasted hand again in her own, and feeling ashamed that she had been out-done in well-doing by one whom she had been induced to believe ill of.

" So Dora isn't a hypocrite, after all," said she, as soon as Anne and herself were in the street again. " I think we have all treated her shabbily, and I, for one, mean to tell her so. I always thought it was strange, if she was all you said she was, that Aunt Daisy should think so much of her."

" You can side with her, if you want to. You'll only get laughed at by the other girls; they know what she is as well as I do," said Anne, with a toss of her head.

" They only know what you told them, I believe; and *I've* got something to tell them, now."

" So you're going to make a great talk about her visiting Sarah Johnson ? "

" I'm going to tell them all about our visit."

" If you do you'll be sorry for it, for I'll have you turned out of the club; so you'll lose a great many good times for nothing; for they all know that she goes there, and they know what she goes there for, too; she only does it to show off, and make folks think she's an angel."

Ella made no reply, for at that moment, as they turned a corner, Lucy and Dora, the inseparable friends, were seen walking towards them, rapidly. Presently the four girls were opposite each other, and the expression on each one's face was worthy of notice. Lucy's round, good-natured face expressed perfect happiness, if ever a face did. Dora's was thoughtful, Ella's troubled, and Anne's expressed proud defiance, as she passed the two without a sign of recognition.

"Where are you going?" said Ella, pausing and addressing them.

"To the widow Johnson's. Want to come?" replied Lucy.

"I've just come from there, but I'll go with you, if you say so."

"Oh, we say so, only you'll have to make yourself useful, if you come; for the widow wouldn't want us to take up her whole kitchen without paying for the use of the room."

"What could I do?" questioned Ella, as she turned and walked beside Lucy.

"I can't tell till we get there. What was the widow doing when you were there?"

"Washing, as usual."

"She must have had a big wash to be so late about it. You and I can help her clear up, while Dora reads to Sarah."

"What?" said Ella, inquiringly. "Clear up?"

"Yes; hang out the last of the clothes, clear away the tubs, and fix the room up spanking nice, while Mrs. Johnson takes home the clothes she washed yesterday."

At that reply Ella's face took on such an expression of consternation that Lucy laughed outright, and Dora, laughing also, said : "I don't think Ella will enjoy going with us, after all."

"I'd get my dress all soiled, wouldn't I, doing such work?" said Ella.

"You can roll up your sleeves, can't you? and Mrs. Johnson will lend you a big apron that you can tie round your neck, an' it will reach to the floor, and so cover your dress all up; but perhaps you'd better turn about and go with Anne; she'd never speak to you again if she should see you in such an apron, that's a fact," said Lucy, laughing at the thought of the contempt that would be visible on Anne's face, if she should see Ella with her sleeves rolled up, and such an apron on, doing the widow Johnson's work. Ella thought of it, too, and some of Lucy's spirit seemed to take possession of her as their eyes met.

"I don't care," said she. "My going with you two now, and leaving her to go home alone is something she won't get over very soon. But I won't care if you and I can be friends."

"As soon as you are Dora's friend, you are mine," replied Lucy.

"I'll not only be Dora's friend, but will try to make all the girls know her, as I know her now, if she has a mind to be good-natured, and forget how shabbily I have treated her."

" *You* treated me shabbily?" inquired Dora. "I didn't know it if you have."

"I took sides with her against you, and voted you out of the club, and believed everything she said about you."

" You wasn't to be blamed for that; she meant to turn all the girls against me, and I knew she would; but it didn't worry me any, as I knew you all must find her out in time. I expect she will change, too, in time, and like me as well as she does anyone, which isn't saying much."

" I don't know about that," said Ella, "I guess she'll never like you as well as she likes Miss Cleverly."

" Who's Miss Cleverly?" questioned Dora.

" Why, haven't you heard about her? She's a friend of Aunt Daisy's, who is visiting her; she was at our club, last evening, and she and Anne became great friends at once. I should have thought Lucy would have told you about her, as you room together. I and Emma talked about her for a long while after we went to bed."

" What was there to talk about?"

" Oh, dear! if you could have seen how she was dressed, you wouldn't ask that! I never saw a girl dressed so richly in my life before."

"Then you may be sure it wasn't Miss Cleverly, that Anne took a liking to, but her clothes," replied Dora. " Miss Cleverly, wouldn't have been noticed by Anne if she had been poorly. dressed, I know. What do you think about it Lucy?"

" I think just as you do. Miss Belle Cleverly in a calico dress would have been beneath Anne's notice."

" Perhaps you are right," said Ella, thoughtfully.

" We'll prove it, some day. But there's Mrs. Johnson at the window! She sees us coming, and she's grinning all over her face, way up into her gray hair! There she goes now, after the aprons!"

" I'm ready for one," said Ella with a laugh.

" You'll say its right down good fun when you get into it. And then to see her old face light up when everything has been done as well as she could do it herself! It's too bad that Sarah isn't a strong girl like one of us!" The latter part of Lucy's sentence was delivered in a low tone that Mrs. Johnson might not hear it, for the three girls had stepped upon the piazza, and, without knocking they opened the door and walked into the kitchen, where Mrs. Johnson greeted them with a smile from behind the wash-tub.

In a very few minutes the girls had sent her away, and taken possession of the room. Dora had brought a book from the Hive Hall library, which was full of pictures. This she gave to Sarah to look at while they were " clearing up." Then Lucy disappeared with the basket of clothes that were ready to hang out, while Dora and Ella cleared away the tubs; by the time that was done Lucy returned, and all three set to work to tidy up the room, while the merry jests at Ella's awkwardness brought a flush of pleasure to the sick girl's cheeks.

When everything was in order, Dora took the book she had brought, and seated herself beside Sarah to read aloud, until Mrs. Johnson returned, which she did in the course of half an hour, looking very grateful for the help her young visitors had given her.

" What kind of a time did you have? " said Lucy to Ella, on their way home.

" A splendid time," replied Ella, with a laugh, as she thought of all that had been done. " If you always have as much fun it's better than going to the club, to go with you."

" Meanwhile Anne walked back to Hive Hall, angry enough, at first, at Ella's desertion, but she soon consoled herself with the thought that the next evening the club would meet, and she would see Miss Cleverly again, whose company was much to be preferred to Ella's, or any of the girls at Hive Hall.

CHAPTER XVII.

A LETTER FROM EDGAR.

"LETTER for Dora Wentworth!" said Mrs. Burns, holding up the epistle in sight of the whole school, as the children were filing out of the recitation room, one afternoon, a few days later.

Dora stepped up to the teacher's desk, as she was passing out, and received it, amid the wondering gaze of all her companions, for it was the first letter that had ever been received by any of them.

"Come up to our room, Rolly!" said she, as she passed into the entry, and ran up stairs, holding the letter as though afraid of wrinkling it.

"Oh, are you going to let me help read it?" said Lucy, delightedly, as she followed her.

"Of course. Here we are! Let's lock the door, so no one can come in while we are read-

ing! I didn't think he'd write so soon, did
you?"

"Who is it from?"

"Edgar Ford."

"Is it? I forgot all about that he was going
to write. Do hurry and let us see what he has
to say!" and Lucy took a seat beside Dora on
the bed, as curious to know what the letter
contained as was the one to whom it was
addressed. After opening it carefully, Dora
began to read as follows:

"DEAR DORA: — I have just finished a letter
to Aunt Daisy, and will write to you, as I
promised to let you know how I liked my present. I think it is splendid! I opened the box
that night, and was very careful to have no one
near when I opened it. I might have saved
myself the trouble. I am using it now, and if
there is more ink on this paper than is necessary
you may know it is caused by my liking to dip
my pen in the ink so often. The likeness is
good, too, and looks like me; only I must say
I think it's a little flattered. But as you made
it, that is to be expected.

I like going to school here very much; and I
like the boys, too, only I have to keep my eyes
open, or they'll get the best of me. The first
night I came, after I had gone to bed, and to

sleep, they came into my room, and tied ropes
to each corner of the sheet, then passed them
over hooks on the wall, and pulled the sheet,
with me in it, way up in the air; then took
away the bed from under me. They did their
work so carefully, that they did not wake me
up, and I might have slept all night, as though
in a hammock, only the sheet was an old one,
and I went through, down — down — into what
I thought was the ocean, but it proved to be
only a wet blanket that they had spread there
for me. I kept my eyes about me in the morning, and the boy that came up to me before
them all, and asked me so politely if I had
slept well, I knew was the one that originated
that little plot, and I have not yet decided how
to reward him for his ingenuity. Perhaps you
can think of some way for me to do that, as
you were always good at thinking of anything
in that line.

I have no time to write more to-day. Think
of some way for me to get even with that boy,
and send your letter in Aunt Daisy's care.

EDGAR FORD.

Hollowcliffe School.

"Are you going to answer it?" said Lucy, as
soon as Dora had finished reading.

"Of course."

"And tell him how he can get even with
that boy?"

" What! after my experience at *getting even?*
It's not likely. I'll write and tell him he'd
better let things be just the way they are, unless
he wants to feel as though he had suddenly
made the acquaintance of all the hornets in a
hornet's nest, and then not have the satisfaction
of killing one. Only rogues should play at
getting even ; good people always get the worst
of it. What do you think Aunt Daisy told me
last night, Rolly?" and Dora, as she spoke,
folded her letter carefully away, then took from
the table a tool and began to work away at the
eyelids on the bust of Aunt Daisy.

"I don't know ; what did she?" said Lucy.

"You couldn't guess if you were to try a
year; so I'll take pity on you, and tell you.
She and Mr. Milly are going to Europe next
year, if nothing happens."

"I've heard of that before."

"But that isn't all. They were both in here
yesterday, it seems, while I was in the school-
room; they came to criticise that," continued
she, with a nod towards the busts ; "and some
one came with them, too."

"Someone? Who do you mean by someone?"

"A real sculptor!" Lucy's round eyes grew rounder, as she looked her surprise, but she made no reply.

"Yes," continued Dora, "a real sculptor! Aunt Daisy said she brought him just to see that. I felt dreadfully when she told me. I wouldn't have cared if it had only been done; but to have him see such eyelids as those were yesterday! I hadn't got the edge done, and they looked more like baker's rolls than they did like eyelids. But Aunt Daisy said that he liked it, and now she says that I'm going to Europe with her, when she goes."

"*You* going to *Europe?*" exclaimed Lucy.

"Yes; going to Italy, where I can study the great masters. She is going to introduce me to some of the famous woman artists, and maybe I'll not come back to America for years."

"Oh, dear! dear!"

"What's the matter?"

"I don't see how you can say anything like that, as though you enjoyed saying it."

"I never enjoyed saying anything so much in my life, and that's the truth, Rolly. The only thing I'm sorry about is that you can't go with me. If you had only stuck to painting as I told you to, you might go to."

"Stuck to painting! Didn't I use up the box of paints that Aunt Daisy gave me for a Christmas present, and no one ever went into ecstacies over anything I ever painted. Aunt Daisy would say, 'that's very good Lucy; very good indeed,'' and that's the last I ever heard about it. I often wonder how she came to say so much, when I look at some of the roses I painted; they look more as though ripe cherries had fallen on the paper and got smashed there, than they looked like roses."

"But you could have done better in time."

"In a lifetime, perhaps, but I don't expect to have but one lifetime, and I wouldn't spend it that way for the world, even if I had mountains of paint to do with as I please."

"Well, Rolly, just as soon as I get rich I'll come back after you, and we'll live together the rest of our lives."

"Perhaps I'll get rich first. If I do I'll go over after you, and put an end to your stone-cutting," replied Lucy, with a laugh.

"Then you've decided on what you're going to be?"

"Yes; I'm going to be a dressmaker. I'm good at sewing, you know, and that's the only thing I am good at. I'd rather be a teacher like Mrs. Burns, only I'm not smart enough, and I don't think it's so profitable, either ; dress-makers make piles of money. Ella is going to be a teacher ; did you know it ?

" No ; is she ? "

" Yes ; so Aunt Daisy is going to give her a better education than she can get here, as she is giving Edgar Ford."

" The other boys are all going to learn trades I suppose."

" Yes ; I heard Aunt Daisy say so."

"I wonder what Anne Porter will be ? "

" A milliner."

" Land ! I might have known without asking. She'll be happy if she has all the laces and rib-bons she wants to trim her hats with. I'll visit her when I come home from Italy, and buy the best hat she has in her store. I'd find all man-ner of fault with it before I bought it, of course," and Dora laughed softly to herself. "Then," continued she, " I'd call on you to get a dress made. You wouldn't know me, of course."

" Wouldn't I ? "

"No ; how could you ? I'd be a woman, you know. I wouldn't let you know who I was till the dress was done, for fear you'd slight it. I

can imagine just how you'd talk to your assis-
tant: 'This dress is for Dora Wentworth; get
it done as soon as you can, and you needn't be
over particular, because she doesn't know the
difference between running and hemming, or
stitching and felling.' "

" That's just the way I'd talk if you'd try
not to make yourself known; for I *should* know
you if you were a woman, and I'd make that
dress set like — like — well, like the skin on
Mrs. Johnson's face; there'd be just as many
wrinkles in it, I can tell you."

" What would I be doing all the time you
were making the dress? "

" You'd be waiting for it to be done, and
thinking I didn't know you."

" That's where you're mistaken. I could tell
at first how that dress was going to set, and if
it didn't suit me, I'd go right to work and make
the awfulest homely bust of you I could make,
out of plaster; then I'd do it up and take it to
you when I went for the dress, and ask you if
you wouldn't be willing to take your pay in
trade, as I really couldn't afford to give money
for such a piece of work."

" I wonder," said Lucy, laughing, " if we
really could do anything like that, if we should

meet after not having seen each other for years."

"It's not likely. I couldn't keep back from rushing at you and shaking you out of your shoes, I know. To-night is club night, isn't it?" questioned Dora, suddenly changing the conversation.

"Yes; and you have no idea, Dora, how much the girls want you to join. Ella has been telling them some of the greatest things about you and me and Anne Porter. They have nearly all turned against Anne, and no wonder, for she is getting to be so unbearably proud since Belle Cleverly makes so much of her, she'll scarcely speak to any of them. They all voted you into the club, yesterday, and were indignant enough with her when she wouldn't give her consent for you to join. They'll turn her out and vote you president, yet, by the way they're going on now."

"For mercy's sake, Rolly, don't let them think of such a thing! if you do, they'll spoil all the fun. Talk to them, and tell them I wouldn't join, anyway; that I've got too much work to do. Keep them quiet till after Christmas, when Miss Cleverly will take her grand departure; then I don't care what they do."

CHAPTER XVIII.

NEVER COMING BACK.

"I DON'T know what I shall do, after you are gone!" The speaker, Anne Porter, was walking up and down the, hall, arm in arm with Belle Cleverly, this Christmas eve, and the last evening of Belle's visit to Aunt Daisy.

The members of the club were scattered in groups all over the hall, talking and laughing together, and perfectly unconscious that their president was very unhappy, indeed. They might not have cared if they had known it, for she had ceased to be a favorite with them, and few took the trouble to look at her as she passed by, arm in arm with Miss Cleverly, who was dressed this evening richer than ever before.

"I'm sure of one thing," continued Anne, "I shall not have anything more to do with this club." 260

" You'll not ? " asked Belle, in some surprise righting her dress by a graceful movement of her disengaged hand.

" No, indeed. I believe I hate every one of them. They haven't a thought above a snail's. A snail doesn't seem to trouble itself much about how it looks, and no more do they."

"A snail couldn't look any better if it tried, could it ? " said Belle, with an attempt at a smile. Laughing aloud was something she never indulged in.

" But *they* could, and that's where they're beneath a snail, I think. Besides, they are beginning to make a fuss because Dora Wentworth isn't allowed to join. I suppose they'll work till they get her in, then, of course, I won't have anything more to do with it."

" I wish I could have seen her before I went."

" You do ? "

" Yes. I'm curious to know what she looks like, I've heard so much about her."

" She's a very common-looking girl, I can assure you. Coarse, and with no more style than a — than a — I don't know what," said Anne, who was not good at thinking of a

similie. "But who did you hear speak of her?
I'm sure I haven't mentioned her since the first
evening you came."

"Daisy and Mr. Milly speak about her occasionally."

"They do?"

"Yes."

"What in the world do they find to say
about her?"

"They were talking yesterday about taking
her to Europe with them."

"Taking her to Europe?" repeated Anne.
"What for?"

"Oh, so she can study, and become a sculptoress; I think that's what they said she was
going to be. Did you ever see any of her
work?"

"Work!" scornfully. "I should call it play!
Yes, I've seen a specimen of what, perhaps, she
calls work," said Anne, thinking of the pig
carved out of wood and labelled Anne Porker,
that she had found in her desk, one morning,
over a year ago.

"What do you think of it?"

"Don't ask me. I'm no judge of such things.
It's my opinion if Aunt Daisy is going to take

her to Europe, she is going to take her there just to get rid of her."

" Do you really think so ?"

" Yes; and I think the sooner she gets her there, the better, too."

" She must be very disagreeable to make you dislike her so."

" She is."

" In what way ? "

" In every way; but I happen to know that she's a hypocrite, which makes her more disagreeable to me."

" Tell me all about how you came to find that out, will you? You speak so positively you must 'have proof. Let's go and sit over there in the corner, where no one will hear what we are talking about. There! now tell how you came to find out she's a hypocrite. I like to listen to anything like that; it's as good as reading a story."

" We never liked each other, from the first of our coming here," began Anne, after the two were seated. " But at first she used to show her dislike plainly enough. She was always ready to say something disagreeable to me, on every occasion; and when she couldn't plague

me by talking, she'd think of something to do,
such as carving out a pig and naming it Anne
Porker, and putting it in my desk; and teaching her parrot to call me names; and putting a
whole nest of young rats in my best hat. I
can't begin to tell you half the disagreeable
things she did, and laughed over, but the greatest of them all was her telling an old gipsy
woman to go into my room and steal my best
hat and dress. I was in my room when the
gipsy came, and she nearly killed me; then she
came back that night, and stole all the children's clothes, but Edgar Ford managed to get
them back again."

"It's a wonder my friend Daisy let her stay
here, after that," said Belle, apparently much
interested.

"Aunt Daisy didn't know she had anything
to do with the gipsy's coming for a long time
afterwards, then she found it out someway; and
what do you think this Dora Wentworth did?
She convinced Aunt Daisy that I was the only
one to blame all the time!"

"I don't see how she could do that."

"Well she did. Everything seemed to happen to help her, too. Don't you think, one day

we were both sent to the village on an errand, and we got caught in a fearful thunder-storm. We went into an old barn for shelter and that was struck by lightning, and we were both knocked senseless. Dora came to first and saw the barn was all on fire, and there was no way to get out except by a small window, as the door was closed by burning timbers; she said she tried to lift me up to the window, but couldn't; then when she saw that the burning roof would soon fall in, she took a red-hot brand and burned my hand with it to bring me to; it *did* bring me to; there's the scar now. I can just remember of crawling through the window, and she after me, then the roof fell in, and I fainted away again."

"Then she was the means of saving your life, after all. I thought somebody said that was all a story made up by her, and you two never went into the barn."

"I was the one that said so, I guess."

"Did you say so?"

"Yes."

"What for?"

"Because I don't like to let her know I think she saved my life."

" You really think she did, don't you ? "

" Oh, yes. If I had been in the barn a minute longer nothing could have saved me, I
know."

" Then why not tell her so ? "

" Because it would gratify her too much."

" I don't see how that could be ; but go on.
You haven't told me yet how you came to know
she was a hypocrite."

" I'm coming to that. After the storm, I was
fearfully sick for a long while; but one day,
when I was getting better, into my room came
Dora, and she asked my pardon for all the mean
things she had ever said or done to me."

" I think that was noble of her."

" I don't."

" You don't ? why ? "

" Because she only did it to show off; and
make Aunt Daisy and the girls think her a
saint, and me a sinner ; for she knew all the
time I wouldn't pardon her, because, knowing
her as I did, I would be sure to think she was
only hatching some new plot to plague me."

" Did you think so ? "

" Yes, of course I did."

" And that was why you wouldn't pardon
her ? "

" Yes; don't speak so loud! I do not want them to hear what we are talking about; and after she went out of my room she went to Aunt Daisy, first, and told her how ungrateful I was after she had saved my life, then she told all the girls about it, and made me out an awful creature."

" But she might have been sincere when she asked your pardon, and might have really wanted to make up with you."

" Ah, no! didn't I hear her tell Lucy Stone, under my window, not ten minutes after that, she was going to turn missionary, with me for the savage, and that she had promised Aunt Daisy that she would make me as good a girl as there was at Hive Hall!"

Belle Cleverly started suddenly, and cried out, as she looked into Anne's face.

" What's the matter?" questioned Anne, solicitously.

" Nothing. I was thinking what a fool she was."

" Who?"

" Why, that Dora Wentworth, to let you hear her say that."

" I was very glad I did hear her, I can tell

you. I knew just how to meet her after that.
I succeeded in turning all the girls against her,
but she managed to make friends with Ella,
lately, and Ella is doing her best to make her
a favorite again. Let her do it. I don't care,
now, for since I've known you there's not one
of them I'd care to have for a friend."

"But you won't have me for a friend after
to-night."

"I shall have you for a friend, if I don't see
you very often. You will visit Aunt Daisy
next year, won't you?"

"No," replied Belle, with a thoughtful
expression on her face, as she turned it towards
the children in the centre of the hall.

"That is strange," said Anne, disappointedly.
"Haven't you had a good time while you've
been here?"

"I never had a better."

"Then why not come again?"

"Because I can't. You will know why before
I go."

"I'm sorry. I was thinking I could look forward to your next visit, if it didn't come for a
year. You are only jesting about not coming
again, I know."

"Belle! Belle!" called Aunt Daisy, at that minute, approaching them. "You take up all the president's time, so she can't attend to her duties. The children are anxious to play something, but they don't know what; can't you or Anne suggest something?"

"Won't there be any reading this evening?" said Belle.

"No; I thought, as it is Christmas eve, we'd better omit the reading this time, and let them do whatever they choose."

"I'm sure I can't think of anything for them to do," said Anne, fretfully, for Belle's information had dampened her spirits for the evening.

"Well, then, Belle, if she can't think of anything we may as well have that transformation scene now, that we were talking about. Anne, Ella, and Emma, I want you all to go in that closet and assure yourselves that there is no other way that one could escape from it but through the door," said Aunt Daisy, opening the closet door mentioned.

"Why, of course we know that there isn't!" said the three girls, looking into Aunt Daisy's face, questioningly.

"Are you quite sure of it?"

"Yes; sure!"

"And are all the other children sure?"

One boy, with more curiosity than the rest, entered the closet to investigate, but came out soon with the information that "he couldn't see any other way out, 'cept through the door."

"And are you sure there is no one in it?" continued Aunt Daisy.

"Course we are! can't we see into every corner?" exclaimed a little girl.

"I want you all to be quite sure both that there is no other way of getting out, and that there is no one in there now, because I'm going to present to you a transformation scene. Come, Belle," and Aunt Daisy gently pushed Belle into the closet, then shut the door and locked it.

For two minutes the children all stood perfectly still, with their eyes on the closet-door, not knowing what to expect. Presently a soft knock was heard inside, and Aunt Daisy opened the door, presenting to view that which caused the members of the reading club to hold their breath in astonishment. They had seen Belle Cleverly, not three minutes before, dressed as only Belle Cleverly could dress, standing where

now stood a very plainly dressed girl! Who
was she? Could she be Belle? and was it possible that dress alone could change her like that,
were some of the thoughts that flashed through
their minds, but they had not time to put them
in words, before Anne, who was standing near
Aunt Daisy, suddenly exclaimed.

"Dora Wentworth!" instantly the other
children took up the cry, and "Dora Wentworth! Dora!" escaped from every mouth in
the hall.

"How did she get there?" "Where is
Belle?" questioned some, who did not understand the affair; but Anne, after one look at
the pile of rich clothing upon the floor, understood it all perfectly, and without another word
she turned and left the hall.

"Dora Wentworth! Was it really you all
the time?" said Ella, who was not yet willing
to admit that she had been so greatly deceived.

"It wasn't anybody else," replied Dora,
emerging from the closet.

"Not even Belle Cleverly!" said Lucy, laughing.

"I was as much deceived as any of the children," said Mrs. Burns. I don't see how she
did it!"

"She did it *cleverly!*" replied Aunt Daisy, with a merry laugh, in which the children joined.

"Lucy, you didn't seem to be surprised at all!" said Ella, looking into the round eyes that had not grown rounder with surprise when the closet door was opened.

"I knew it all the time; that's why," was the reply.

"Then it was mean enough in you not to tell *me*, when we were such friends."

"I had promised not to, that's why I didn't; but I wanted to, ever so many times; especially when you said that Belle Cleverly was better-looking than Dora Wentworth.

"Well, she was. I won't take that back, anyway."

"Oh, it's all the same now, whether you do or not," said Lucy, laughing as usual.

"Where's Anne?" interrogated Aunt Daisy, who had just become aware of Anne's absence.

"True enough! where's the president?" said Ella, looking over the hall.

"She's gone after Belle Cleverly!" said a bright-appearing girl, and the remark caused a general laugh, for all knew the feeling that existed between Anne and Dora, and they could partly imagine what a state of mind Anne must be in at that minute.

Dora's eyes sought Aunt Daisy's for a moment, then without a word she left the hall and proceeded towards Anne's room.

She opened the door softly, but could see nothing, as there was no lamp burning there, and the room was as dark as a moonless night could make it.

Guided by the sound of stifled sobs, Dora crossed the room, and laid a hand softly upon Anne's shoulder.

"Who is it?" said the latter, starting suddenly, and swallowing a sob.

"It is I—Dora."

"How dare you come in here? I should think you'd be contented with what you've done for to-night!" and Anne was now too angry to sob.

"What have I done that's very dreadful? Come, Anne! you liked me as Belle, why not like me as Dora, and let's be friends; it's time we were, I'm sure."

"Dora Wentworth, I *hate* you! What have you done! You have made me the laughing-stock of the whole school and village, too!"

" I don't think so."

" No, you know it!"

" If I have, it will be easy to turn the laugh on them. All you'll have to do is to go back to the hall with me, and treat me just as you have treated Belle Cleverly. They'll think, then, that you knew it all the time."

" Are you going out of this room, Dora Wentworth?"

" Not till I've explained two or three things, anyway. It's all a mistake, Anne, all the way through. I was mistaken in you, and you in me, especially when you think I wasn't sincere when I asked your pardon that time. I was; for I was truly sorry for what I had done; and I thought you knew it, too, but was too mean to pardon me after I had asked it of you. How was I to know that you mistrusted my motive? and it was no great wonder I called you a savage, was it?"

" I don't want to hear any of your explanations! If you'll leave me alone, in my own room that's all I'll ask of you."

" Anne, you're foolish! You'll only just make yourself the laughing-stock of them all?"

" Let them laugh! What do I care? I hate them all, nearly as much as I hate you!"

" It's a shame, Anne, that we two can't be as good friends all the time, as we were while I was Belle Cleverly."

" Where did you get all those fine clothes? "

" Aunt Daisy got them for me."

" She knew all about it? "

" She was the one that told me to do it. Where are you going? " for Anne had arisen, and was groping in the dark for the door.

" Where are you going? " repeated Dora, on receiving no answer.

" Do you think I'm going to stay longer in the same room with you? " replied Anne, at last, hotly.

" Oh, if that's all, I'll go, and you can stay." With that Dora brushed by Anne in the dark, ran down stairs, and entered the hall again.

" Well? " said Aunt Daisy, questioningly, going up to her as she entered.

" It's just as I expected it would be ; its useless to think that she and I will ever be friends."

CHAPTER XIX.

CONCLUSION.

ALL the scholars but Anne had assembled early in the dining-room, the next morning, waiting for Aunt Daisy to make her appearance and open the door to the room in which was the wonderful Christmas tree.

"It's my opinion," said Dora, who was seated on a window-seat, keeping a sharp lookout down the road for Daisy. "It's my opinion Anne won't feel comfortable when she comes in. Let's all see if we can't treat her just as though nothing had happened."

A general laugh from the scholars followed this speech.

"I, for one, am going to ask her if she does not think you did it well," said Lucy."

"No, don't! I am sure Aunt Daisy would not like to have you allude to it again," entreated Dora.

" Well, then, let's only say, whenever we do anything well, we did it *cleverly*," said Emma Goodwin, with a laugh.

" See here, girls, we were all mistaken in Anne, every one of us, and I most of all. I didn't understand her any better than she understood me. The reason she wouldn't pardon me that time, was because she didn't think I was sincere in asking her pardon. She thought I was planning some new way to plague her, while I thought she refused because she was so mean. Now, I'll tell you what! you have all wanted me to carve your bust for you, but I couldn't carve all, so I didn't carve any. Now, I'll agree to carve a splendid bust of the one who succeeds the best in treating Anne just as though nothing unusual had happened. Here she comes! Look sharp, now, for I'm watching you!"

Aunt Daisy and Anne, the latter looking proud and distant, entered the school-room very soon after Dora finished speaking, and presently the door that had been watched so impatiently by the scholars, was opened.

It would be useless to try to describe that Christmas tree and the presents that were on it, and around it; and impossible to picture the joy the children of Hive Hall felt as the gifts were bestowed upon them by Aunt Daisy; but most of my young readers will be able to understand it all, from their own experience.

Anne was made glad by the present of a handsome new dress, and within an hour she began to show signs of what the girls called "coming round," and they did their best to encourage her.

Later in the day Dora was surrounded by a demonstrative group of children, each one of which claimed the right to that bust she had promised to make.

"I can't decide which one deserves it the most," said she, good-naturedly; "suppose you draw lots to see who shall have it."

"That would be a mean way," said Ella. "Those who didn't do anything would stand as good a chance of getting it, as those who really exerted themselves. Didn't I —"

"I know you did," interrupted Dora, "but two or three others did as well."

"Draw lots, I say!" said Emma Goodwin, who had done nothing but grin.

"That's the only way to settle it," said Lucy.

"Let's wait till Anne comes back, and let her draw, too," for Anne had left the room a minute before.

"We'll agree to that," said Ella, laughing. "I'll cut strips of paper enough, and the one who draws the shortest will be the lucky one."

A piece of paper was soon produced, and the strips were arranged ready for drawing when Anne returned.

"You are just in time, Anne," said Ella. "Dora has promised to make a handsome bust of one of us, and will give it to the one she makes it of. We are going to draw lots, now, to see whose she will make. Come, girls, everything is ready. Who's going to draw first?" Four or five strips were instantly drawn by as many different hands, but the short strip was not among them.

"There, now," exclaimed Ella, "I guess you all wish you hadn't been in such a hurry, but had waited till your turns came properly. Here, Anne, you are the best-behaved one here! you can draw next."

"I don't care about it," said Anne, folding her arms, and looking at the strips of paper Ella held before her.

" Oh, yes! draw! just for the fun of it!" urged Ella; and Anne, thinking she would not be very likely to draw the short strip, complied.

" The short strip!" " The short strip!" " Anne has got it!" was the shout that followed, as she looked at the paper she had drawn.

"Any one can have it that wants it. I'm sure I don't care for it," said she, when the noise had partly subsided.

" Oh, no! nobody else wants it," interposed Lucy. " You drew it, fair and square, and Dora is bound to carve a handsome bust of you, and give it to you. Don't say anything more about it till you see it; then if you don't want it my name isn't Lucy Stone!"

Aunt Daisy, entering at that moment, put a stop to the conversation.

" Wasn't it odd," said Lucy, that night, to Dora, after they had gone to their room and were preparing to retire, looking very tired indeed, after the excitement of the day. " Wasn't it odd that Anne should draw that short strip."

" Odd enough."

" If I were you I'd flatter that bust."

"I was thinking about that. I've tried for over a year to be friendly with Anne for Aunt Daisy's sake, and nothing I could do would please her. But that bust is what's going to do it! I'll make it a great deal better-looking than she is, then if she doesn't think as much of me ever after, as she thought of Belle Cleverly, I'm mistaken in her, that's all."

Time proved that Dora was not mistaken in her. The bust was finished to perfection, and presented to Anne, who warmed towards Dora immediately upon receiving it. She takes such good care of it, that it will, doubtless, be as perfect as ever when she is old, and bent, and wrinkled; then, perhaps, on Christmas days, when she is surrounded by her grandchildren, she will take it out to show them how she looked when she was a girl.

Time did more than prove Dora was not mistaken in Anne. It drove all the children, one after another, from Hive Hall, and scattered them far and wide, but not before they were made strong enough to take up their life-work without faltering.

One more scene, and then our story is ended.

It was Christmas eve, ten years later; and Hive Hall was ablaze with light, for its former inmates always have a "reunion" there, on that evening. It was yet early, and young men and women were continually arriving; but ten years had worked such a change with them it would be hard to recognize any of them as our old friends.

They were assembled in the large room that was formerly used as a school-room, and all seemed to be talking, laughing, shaking hands, and congratulating each other. But one couple had separated from the others and seated themselves in a remote corner of the room; we will try to get near enough to hear what they say, and perhaps we can recognize them by their conversation.

"If I go back to Italy—" were the first words audible, spoken by the lady, who had our old friend Dora's laughing eyes.

"If you go back!" repeated the gentleman, whose bearded face we do not remember seeing before.

" Yes; if I go back, I'll—"

"But I thought I said in my last letter you must not go back!"

"Did you?" with a little laugh, "you always were famous for saying unreasonable things, Edgar Ford! Doesn't Aunt Daisy look handsome to-night?"

"Yes; she's coming this way. Shall I tell her we have decided to be married in the spring?"

"There you are, unreasonable again! What is to become of my art, and all my dreams of fame?"

"Your art will live all the same, I'll give you my word; and as for your dreams of fame, we can grow famous together; its ever so much the best way."

We could not hear Dora's reply, but know that, in the spring, there was a wedding at Hive Hall, in which they were the chief actors.

Aunt Daisy is a middle-aged woman now, with boys and girls of her own, and nephews and nieces, too, as large as the children who first appeared at Hive Hall; and every Christmas she has them all together at the Hall, with the men and women who still call her "Aunt," and their children; and a merry time they have.

Every year she is more and more convinced

that Hive Hall was a success, as she beholds how prosperous and happy those who were its inmates are, and compares them to what they might have been, had its doors never been opened to receive them.